TURNED EARTH

To MOLLY,
MAY YOUR THUMBS
ALWAYS BE GREEN!

-DAVID
THE GOOD-

Books by David The Good

General Gardening
Start a Home-Based Plant Nursery

Florida Gardening
Totally Crazy Easy Florida Gardening
Create Your Own Florida Food Forest
Florida Survival Gardening

The Good Guides
Compost Everything
Grow or Die
Push the Zone
Free Plants for Everyone

The Good Ideas
Grocery Row Gardening

Jack Broccoli Novels
Turned Earth
Garden Heat

a Jack Broccoli novel

TURNED EARTH

DAVID T. GOOD

Turned Earth: A Jack Broccoli Novel
David T. Good

Good Books Publishing
goodbookspub.com

ISBN: 978-1-955289-06-1

CONTENTS

PROLOGUE

Dr. John Leighton could not remember how he ended up in the tortoise pen at the Zoological and Botanical Gardens wearing nothing but a straw hat and a modesty gourd, but he certainly was not going to pose for a photograph as the small cluster of Korean tourists seemed to desire.

He was a soil scientist, for goodness sake—not an orangutan! At least he thought he was a soil scientist. A tortoise eyed him mournfully as if in doubt.

Everything was confused. Leighton shook his head and looked around, noticing a tall fence to the left of him behind a stand of bamboo. If he could get over it, he could perhaps find a taxi and get home. Yes, that was the key. If he could remember where his home was, of course. But one step at a time. He grasped the chainlink and painfully climbed upwards towards the top. The wire bit into his bare feet, but he felt strangely detached from his body. There were faraway shouts and gasps behind him but they didn't seem important. At the top of the fence, he almost fell but managed to hold on, his heart thumping and his hands sweating. Carefully, he lowered himself down to the other side of the fence. Some people in uniforms were shouting at him from over the top of a wall now, waving and yelling.

They must not want him to call a taxi, he thought. He'd show them. He'd call the best taxi in the world as soon as he figured out how to find his way out of this maze. At least there were no more tortoises in this part of the gardens. As he skipped through a stand of heliconia, he passed a scratched glass gazing ball and was horrified to see that his face was smeared with paint. Or was that *blood* around his mouth?

Vaguely he remembered pulling at a hard carapace and gnawing on something scaly, but that had been a dream.

He hoped it was a dream. The modesty gourd was giving him nerves, though. He was sure he had never owned a modesty gourd. Dr. Shemer—his nemesis from the Anthropology Department—was the only person he knew for certain had one, and that only because Dr. Shemer had worn it to class a few times before some hyper-sensitive freshman (freshwoman?) had reported him for harassment.

This gourd didn't look like Dr. Shemer's, though. It was likely a different species. Shemer's was a common *Lageneria sicerari*—heck, he probably got it from the Amish—but if his somewhat blurry, non-bespectacled eyesight could be trusted, it had been crafted from a carefully managed and bound fruit of *Crescentia cujete*.

But where had he gotten it, and why was he here?

He stared at his reflection in the sphere, and he began to remember something else from the night before. The lab, the parking lot, a short man in black—there was no reason to be wearing this ridiculous outfit, especially in public! And there was most certainly no reason for a tiger to be crouching, reflected in the ball, just to the lower left of his wildly distorted arm.

No reason at all.

CHAPTER ONE

Five feet across always seemed excessive to Jack Broccoli. He was convinced Jeavons had added an extra twelve inches just to be contrary. *Microclimates my foot*, he thought. It didn't matter, though, Jack was all about the four-foot wide beds. Darn *Grow More Vegetables*—full speed ahead!

Though full speed at double-digging was easier said than done.

It was March in Virginia, but it already felt like mid-July. Jack was half-way through this particular bed and his shirt was soaked through, clinging to his well-formed physique. He thought about ripping it off, then remembered the last time he had done so. His next-door neighbor's dumpy wife had wandered over to the fence and made eyes at him while talking about her depression issues, insomnia, mother-in-law, attempts to get pregnant, struggle finding a minivan that fit their budget in case she got pregnant and had another child which would necessitate purchasing said minivan, fear of getting pregnant, and the infection on her calf that had never quite gone away after, if he remembered correctly, she got a butterfly tattoo. *But wasn't it cute though?*

Jack's shirt was staying on.

He started inverting a new row of sod into the trench he'd just finished. Two-thirds done now. Working in the garden was a good break from working at his job.

He had moved here for the job the previous summer, from three states away, and it had been too late in the year to plant more than a small fall garden of fava beans and kale. His boss was a great guy— an old friend of his father's. Arnold Hardin and Jack Broccoli Sr.

4

TURNED EARTH

had served together on special missions for F.O.R.E.S.T.—the Forestry Operations Reserve Espionage Strike Troops. When Jack was twelve, his father disappeared during a mission in Africa, and Hardin had brought the news back to Jack, his mom, and his brother Drew.

Hardin stepped into Jack's life like an uncle. Since Hardin and his wife were unable to have children of their own, their relationship with the Broccoli Boys had been almost parental, albeit from a few states away. On summers and long weekends and holidays, the families got together.

When Jack finished college and Hardin needed a new guy for his soil sampling business, a match was made. Now here Jack was, digging up the back yard of his very own house, working an honest job (though if he had to admit it, he was getting bored) and bringing home the bacon. The house was a little over his head price-wise, but it was in a good neighborhood. And at age 24, he was doing well for himself.

Jack mopped sweat off his brow as he knocked out the last few trenches of soil. If he didn't get this bed of turnips in soon they'd bolt. Granted, it wasn't the first bed of turnips he'd planted this spring. It was his fourth. Jack appreciated the functional solidity of turnips.

The first bed had the standard Purple Top White Globe. Though it was pedestrian, it was always a good producer. The next bed had an ancient variety from Japan known as "Hinona Kabu". They were long and thin, almost like a carrot in shape but with the purple and white coloration common to many turnips. He had grown them the previous two years and they were quite good.

The third bed had the most interesting type, a new addition this year. It was an ancient and rare Finnish heirloom, according to Jack's friend Niklas. They shared seeds back and forth, carefully concealing them in birthday cards, books, and even the handle of a trowel once. If you didn't hide seeds well, they were confiscated at the border. These had arrived inside a small wooden figurine of a stylized bear. A little label inside denoted them as "Kiikala turnip". Jack had given them extra care. He'd already decided to dedicate a third of the Kiikala bed to seed production and harvest all the other turnips before they bloomed so they didn't cross. If they were as rare as Niklas claimed it was well worth the extra effort. He could put some seeds in the freezer and save others to give away.

He had not decided yet what type of turnips to plant in the last bed, but he didn't want to plant more Purple Top White Globes, and that was the only type available locally. Jack was in the mood for something exotic.

As Jack drove his spade into the clay again, he heard a familiar voice from next door. The other next door from Tattoo Infection Girl, that is.

"Pak Choi!" he yelled. "I thought you were gone until summer!?"

A middle-aged Chinese man looked over the fence and smiled. "No, Jack. Plans changed. What are you doing so much digging for?"

Jack had met Pak after buying his house. He was away a lot, but when he was home, Pak was often working in his garden. After Jack had commented positively on Pak's collection of potted *Adenuim obesum* specimens, the two had become closer than acquaintances, if not quite friends.

Jack grinned. "Turnips, Pak. More Turnips." Pak shook his head sadly. "What?" Jack said. "What's wrong with turnips?"

"Not turnips, Jack. I am not offended by your strange enthusiasm for an unappealing root vegetable. It is your decidedly unfriendly approach to soil."

Pak had made the arguments for no-till gardening so many times that if Jack hadn't bought into it by now, he never would.

"Not the no-till argument again, Pak. If you could have convinced me you would have by now. You might like that 'living lightly' stuff, but anyone worth their salt works the earth."

Pak made a rude noise and disappeared. A few moments later, Jack heard the sound of running water, then a pause, and then a bubbling sound.

He shrugged and went back to digging.

∗ ∗ ∗

The cool morning air whipped through Jack's hair as he drove into town in the 1971 carrot-top green 429 Super Cobra Jet Mustang Mach 1 which he'd converted to run on his own special formulation of high octane vegetable oil. He loved driving with the windows down and smelling the dew and fresh grass scent of the countryside.

Jack popped an *Ocean Octaves!* seaweed crisp into his mouth. As he munched, he rebuked himself yet again for eating the confounded things. *They contain both gluten and soy, Jack. The former isn't good for the gut—the latter drops your testosterone.* On a quick impulse he threw the entire bag of *Ocean Octaves!* out beside the road. He breathed a sigh of relief and kept driving for 36 seconds.

At 37 seconds the guilt of littering hit him. He braked hard, pulled off the road into the grass, turned around, then drove back to pick up the bag of *Ocean Octaves!* It took him a minute or so to spot it in the tall grass, but he did. Angrily he threw them into the passenger seat and pulled his car back onto the road.

By the time he got to the office, he'd eaten the rest of the bag.

The heavy glass entry door closed behind Jack. Between him and the lab entrance sat a gracelessly aging wood and laminate desk. Behind the desk sat Angie. She was on the phone, as usual.

Despite her extra weight, she had a face as angular as an F-117. He knew she had cats because she smelled very slightly of litter boxes. That and she always talked about her cats. He thought she might have a son, too, but Angie never mentioned him. Just cats. Cats who had exacting taste in cat food brands. Cats who never learned what things should be scratched and what things should not be. Cats who experienced explosive diarrhea when they weren't fed to their exacting taste in cat food.

"Hi Angie," said Jack.

Angie waved cheerfully. Like all women, she had a thing for Jack. Jack wished she didn't, but he kept it to himself. She was a member of the team—though he knew no one liked her, except maybe her cats.

He had almost made it to the lab door when she hung up the phone with a loud sigh.

"That was the vet, Jack."

Jack nodded, his hand reaching for the door knob.

"Remember Squiggles?"

Jack didn't.

"Squiggles knocked some laundry detergent into his Fancy Feast. All weekend I couldn't figure out why he kept foaming."

Jack was already tired of this.

"Out of his bottom."

Jack raised an eyebrow.

"He might die," Angie said.

"I hope not," Jack lied.

He gripped the door knob. It was smooth, cool, and comforting in his hand. The door knob would set him free, if only he turned it and walked through the portal it controlled. On the other side was a wonderful, Angie-free place, with nary a mention of fizzing feline fannies.

"Nibbles also ate some of it."

Jack started to turn the knob.

"He didn't send it out the back end, like Squiggles, though."

Jack turned the knob further.

"Instead, he was at the table and let out a huge burp."

Jack didn't know cats could burp.

"But as he did, a big soap bubble came out of his mouth. It was the size of a basketball and it stuck to his whiskers! I felt so bad for him!"

Click. The latch released. Jack swung the door open and stepped through.

"Oh, Jack," Angie exclaimed, "I'm not done!" But the door clicked shut behind him before he could hear any more about sick cats. He had done it. He was free. Well, not really free. He still had to work an eight-hour day, but at least he had made it through the reception area.

Raman was already sitting at the accessions desk, fingers clicking over the keyboard as he added numbers and details to the ever-growing list of samples being received from around the country. "Hi Raman," Jack said.

Raman nodded at him, distantly. He was always distant, except when talking about the nice things he owned. In the main work area, Bill had already fired up the drying oven and was placing sample trays into neat rows on the rack. Bill was a paunchy older guy with thinning hair who had been working in soil labs since the 70s. "Hey Jack, how are you bud?" he said. "Have a good weekend?"

"Better than Angie's, apparently," Jack replied.

Bill laughed. "Angie never has a good anything, Jack."

Jack nodded. "Can cats belch, Bill?"

Bill shook his head. "I don't think so."

"I didn't think so either."

Bill looked thoughtful. "They can yack things up, though. Hairballs and such. Like owls, I think."

Jack remembered that about owls. But it wasn't their own hair they yakked up, he thought. It was the remnants of their prey, owls not having hair.

"If cats could belch, could one, say, blow a big bubble by eating laundry detergent and then belching?"

"No, I don't think so."

Jack pushed the whole thing out of his head and gathered his first sample of the day. It was a brownish clay loam, and judging by its friability, the soil possessed a decent organic matter content. He fired up the grinder and fed it in.

Soon he'd do something more with his day-to-day life. Maybe he'd be a researcher for a big corporation run by a gardening enthusiast, trekking through the rainforest in search of heirloom vegetable varieties grown in tiny, isolated villages while fighting poachers, and communists, and mercenaries hired by shady oil prospectors. Plenty more exciting than working here.

Jack of the Jungle. That had a ring to it. He'd drink chicha beside a fire with a group of naked tribesmen who were excitedly passing around roots and gourds they'd grown, sharing seeds with Jack and introducing him to ancient farming techniques involving ironwood shovels and flint pitchforks. Then there would be dancing, of course, with native girls wearing grass skirts with big hoops in their ears, cavorting madly around a fertility god shaped like a pumpkin. They'd make eyes at him, and he would wink at the pretty ones and smile comfortingly at the others. Then the chief would make a speech declaring Jack pukka sahib and give all of the girls to him as wives, and they'd start a little farm and a security outfit. Would turnips grow in Ecuadoristan or one of those other hot countries down there? He would try, that's for sure.

Then, while Jack was lost in visions of the near future, something exciting happened. The grinder emitted a shrill shrieking sound and stopped turning. Smoke suddenly curled alarmingly from the engine just as Jack mashed down the off switch.

Bill rubbed his ears. "Whoa, Jack! what you doing over there?"

"Not sure, Bill—it just started shrieking at me."

"Did you sift the sample first?"

"No, I didn't. My fault."

"Let's hope Hardin didn't hear that sound." Though Hardin liked Jack personally, he was also an exacting and unforgiving man who prided himself on the excellent results obtained in his lab—and the high quality and modernity of his equipment. If anything, he was harder on Jack than on his other employees.

"Me too," said Jack, remembering the time Hardin had threatened to dump him into a vat of $C_6H_{15}NO_5S$, and Jack had replied "I bet that would really sting," and Hardin had shaken his head and stomped off.

Bill took the funnel off the sample grinder and tipped it over into his hand. Out dropped a brilliant metal sphere the size of a shooter marble, somewhat scarred by the action of the machine.

"Well, I'll be." He handed the ball to Jack. "That's your problem right there."

Jack held it up for a closer look. It wasn't just a ball bearing. In the bright fluorescent light of the lab he could see two bearded faces carved on it.

The door to the lab swung open, and Hardin said in his sharp New Jersey accent, "What was that sound?"

"It was me, Mr. Hardin," Jack said, surreptitiously dropping the sphere in his pocket.

Hardin frowned at him. "Either you brought an Oldsmobile with failing brake pads to a halt in here, or you were breaking one of my machines."

"Not intentionally, sir, but if it's broken, I'll pay for it. It was my fault."

Hardin looked at the disassembled soil grinder on the counter. "Did you pull it to bits before or after it started shrieking?"

"After. I forgot to sift the soil first."

"Better hope it works when you put it back together again, Jack. That machine costs eight hundred and forty-nine dollars, plus tax and shipping. Much cheaper than many of our machines, but I assume losing close to a grand might still hurt your wallet a bit, would it not?"

"It would, sir."

"Fix it if you can and be quick about it. We're losing time and money now."

Jack nodded.

Hardin sighed. "You know, I hoped you'd do better than this. I'm leaving for ABA shortly and it seems I have no guarantee of coming back to a lab with working machines in it. Not to mention pop machines."

How was I supposed to know that trying to remove a dollar bill with a screwdriver could cause a short? Anyone could have made that mistake. Besides, it's a stupid design that eats bills then breaks when customers try to retrieve them. I hate that machine. But I also hate to let Hardin down.

"Mr. Hardin, I–"

"No, I don't want excuses. I want hard work. This is your last warning, Jack—no more mistakes."

"Mr. Hardin–"

But Hardin was already gone.

* * *

There were approximately 27 minutes of light left by the time he got home that evening. Just enough time to dig a new 4' x 4' bed, provided he attacked fast. Jack picked a spot where he had dumped a big pile of leaves the previous year. He considered using it for yet another bed of turnips, then decided that he'd better do something else for a change. Maybe beans this time. They'd fix some nitrogen, and he could follow them with turnips in the fall.

He stuck his spade into the ground with a violent thrust. Just as it hit the ground, he heard a muffled yelp. Jack looked both ways. Nothing in sight. He took another chop.

"Yeeeeaow!"

Jack looked around again. He thought the sounds had come from Pak's yard, but all he saw in that direction was his 4' white fence and a slightly taller compost bin just behind it. Once again, he picked up his spade and plunged it into the moist earth.

"YeeeoooooeeeeeoooooWWwwwWWW!" came a sound like that of a cat being given an unexpected bath.

Turning around, Jack now saw Pak pop his head up from behind his compost bin. "Pak, what the heck was that? Why are you yelping?"

"It wasn't me, Jack."

"It wasn't?"

"No, Jack. It was the voice of the fungal community you are destroying, crying out in great pain."

"Oh c'mon, Pak, for goodness sake!" Jack exclaimed.

Pak shook his head sadly and walked away.

That guy, Jack thought, then chuckled. *He may be nuts, but he sure is funny.*

It took another fifteen minutes to dig the bed. Jack could barely make out the edges of the last trench as he filled it in, but he felt satisfied. He went inside to take a shower and find something to eat.

I really should have changed out of my work clothes, he thought, as he looked at a new stain on the side of his khakis. He rifled through his pockets, dumping wallet, keys, pocketknife and a couple of crumpled dollar bills and change on the bathroom counter.

Tunk, click, click, click!

Something heavy bounced off the counter, fell to the floor, skittered across the tile, and rolled behind the toilet. The metal sphere. Jack had forgotten all about it.

He threw his pants into the hamper and dropped to his hands and knees. As he groped around in the narrow space behind the toilet, he thought about how strange it was that spiders liked to live behind toilets in weird, tangly webs.

Not nice webs like the perfect ones you find in meadows. No: dusty, awful-looking webs. Indoor webs are the worst, and the spiders look sick. Long-limbed with grotesquely round abdomens. It's like the indoors are spider slums, inhabited by the Spiders of Walmart. What do they even eat back here?

He finally found the sphere nestled in the dust and webs exactly behind the base of the toilet.

The light in the bathroom was somewhat dim, as Jack had unscrewed all but one of the five 40-watt bulbs lined up in a dressing-room style fixture above the mirror over the sink. The last bulb might actually be a 25-watt, come to think of it.

It's not like I have money to throw around, especially since I'm still a little broke from the custom eco-leather seats I installed in the Mustang. They were made from laminated cornstalk fibers, which Jack thought was awesome. *Not that I have anything against traditional leather. I just like plants and all their works.*

Jack reached up and screwed in two additional bulbs, figuring the fraction of a cent the electricity would cost wasn't worth worrying about at this important juncture.

The sphere was still warm from his pocket. Despite the gouge in one side, he could now quite clearly see two bearded faces on it, one on either side, like anthropomorphic continents rising from a chrome sea. One face looked Oriental, with a long face and thin whiskers. The other face was European, fierce and thickly bearded. Jack knew he'd seen it before. In tiny letters was an inscription: "Everything is everywhere, but the environment selects." *Weird. Is that the new Nike slogan?* Jack put the sphere back on the counter—behind his wallet this time, so it wouldn't take a joyride into the spider slum again—then stepped into the shower.

His thoughts drifted as he showered. Jack wished he could walk away from his job and get right to the chicha and jungle women, but he knew that wouldn't pay nearly enough for his 30-year mortgage on the house. He needed to keep the house, and that meant keeping Hardin happy and not making any more mistakes.

He remembered his Dad once telling him when he was a boy that the best way to confuse and often reconcile an enemy to yourself was an unexpected gift. Jack had tried this once on a co-worker at the agricultural extension he used to work part-time for, back when he was getting his degree.

Larry was a tubby little man who was constantly drinking frothy, sweet espresso drinks from the corner coffee joint. Jack had borrowed Larry's laptop one afternoon so he could get some work done while he was waiting for paperwork at an office in the next county over. When he was back in the office, Jack had turned it over to the IT department without asking Larry first. No harm meant, of course: it was sitting on Jack's desk and the IT nerd had asked, "This one get updated yet?" Jack had said no, then given it to him without thinking.

It turned out that Larry had been compiling a detailed and lengthy list of offenses committed against him by others in the office. Twenty

three people were represented, none with any redeeming features. The
IT nerd found it on the computer and emailed it to everyone in the
office.

It read, in part:

BETH:

*Thinks she is smart. Is not smart. In fact dumb as brick. Fat but
thinks is not.*

*June 17: Misspelled my name on birthday cake as Jerry, told me she
didn't know I hated mouse in old cartoon but she knew.*

*August 20: Threw out my lunch in the fridge. Said was old. Was
not old, was from day before and had not been eaten yet. She knew.*

August 22: Ate last donut was supposed to be mine. She knew.

*September 8: Wore skirt with hula girl hidden in pattern, despite
policy prohibiting provocative clothing. She knew.*

*September 21: Overheard BETH say I was "creepy" when talking
with Deborah in kitchen. When I confronted her she said she didn't
know I was listening. She knew.*

JACK:

Cocky, unreliable, young, stupid.

*June 5: Took my parking space. Said he did not know it was mine.
He knew. Have always parked there.*

*August 3: Wore aftershave that irritated allergies. Warned him
before but he said he didn't know. He knew.*

*October 2: Ate raw garlic at desk and made office smell bad. Said
he had a cold. Knows I am allergic to garlic. Pretended not to know.*

Though Larry was a government employee and not easily fired, he
did receive a thorough dressing down from the boss, and he was sent
to a mandatory "Getting Along with Others" class. Larry hated Jack

after that, and though he didn't say anything, he always stared daggers at him. *And the garlic allergy thing was ridiculous. Everyone should eat raw garlic when they got sick. It's practically a vitamin.*

Jack decided to buy him a coffee one day, to confuse and possibly reconcile his enemy to himself. Larry was sitting at his desk when Jack walked in. As soon as he saw Jack he inhaled sharply and hissed, "Get out!"

"I brought you a gift," Jack said, "Here!"

He stepped forward, iced coffee in hand, but at the last moment his foot caught on the corner of the frayed carpet beneath Larry's desk. He stumbled and smashed the cup on the desk. The older man screamed as the cold coffee spattered him and soaked his papers, and ice cubes bounced everywhere.

Jack assessed the situation and realized a quick retreat was advisable, so he backed out and cautiously shut the door behind him in case Larry wanted to start a fight. He had no desire to break the guy in half. Jack had been barely twenty then, but he spent most of his free time at the gym and looked like it.

Larry later claimed Jack had assaulted him with a deadly weapon. "Broccoli knew I was lactose intolerant!" he had said. "And how much I hate sudden chills! And that I was running late on a project. HE KNEW!"

Jack hadn't known, but that didn't save him from a trip to a "Getting Along with Others" class of his own. He quit the job before lunch on the second day of the three-day event, though, so he never found out whether he would be able to get along with others. Most of the people you were supposed to get along with, according to the instructors, were minorities in wheel chairs. Jack had only known one minority in a wheel chair before, and he wasn't sure if she had actually been a minority, or was just claiming to be one. *What do Pacific Islanders even look like?* He was pretty sure they didn't have red hair and manicured sky blue fingernails.

Jack turned off the water and stepped out of the shower. As he toweled off, he returned to his previous train of thought. He needed to

do something nice to help Hardin and—this was the important part—
not screw it up.

He wrapped the towel around his waist and went to the kitchen. On
top of the fridge was an unopened bag of *Ocean Octaves!*

No, Jack, he thought. *No.*

He grabbed a Celery Stout from the fridge, popped the top, sat
down at his desk and flipped open his MacBook, then typed a search
into DuckDuckGo: *good gift for a boss*

He read a few lists, quickly deciding that a wireless eye massager
was a dumb idea, as was a "deep sea sand art" paperweight. Then he
thought, *Hey, what about a Dilbert collection?* That comic strip took
place in an office, and he remembered it being funny when he read it as
a young teenager. He clicked over to Amazon and bought a paperback
collection. *Why not?* It cost only $6.97 plus shipping, in "very good
condition", sold by Goodwill Industries Sacramento.

He stuffed a handful of *Ocean Octaves!* into his mouth, then looked
down in surprise at the bag in his lap. It was almost empty.

CHAPTER TWO

Dr. Jeremy Freeman had been in Arizona for only a week when he ate the soup. It had been really good soup, he remembered. He had even remarked on it at the time. But then things went blurry. A jellyfish with dreadlocks brought the check, and his host paid, and led him outside to the back of a spaceship—and now he was here. Somehow. In the desert.

He had come from Washington State to work on the Soil Desalination Initiative as a consultant. He loved consulting gigs, as they paid better than his regular work, plus he got his name on the web as a "very important person" in yet another corporate board.

At some point between the desert and the restaurant he had been in a building. The men had been talking about him. They had asked him questions, he thought, and he had answered. Or maybe that was a dream. He thought he remembered walking in the night and being cold.

He usually had excellent recall.

The chill of the desert night was already gone. So was his shirt, and he wondered what had happened to it. Freeman felt very hot. *It's early morning,* he thought, *and the sun has only really just gotten started.*

Water. Water would be really good.

He looked back and saw short stretches of his footprints in the earth, in places where it wasn't rock or hard packed dirt. It was impossible to tell how far he had come, or from what original direction. He couldn't even remember how long ago he had woken from his stupor to find himself in the desert. He could tell from his fatigue and sore feet that he had been walking for long time.

Freeman wasn't used to physical exertion. He was really sweating now. What a day. Or multiple days. He wondered vaguely what his wife was doing right now. *Probably getting her hair and nails done*, he thought. She would have some free time without him around.

The desert flora and fauna were quite different from the life where he lived in Washington near the Pacific. Lots of rainfall there. Big ferns, trees, long, slimy slugs—it was damp. Here everything conserved water.

Water is a really good idea. But where in the world will I find it out here?

He should know the plants out here but he didn't. He'd always spent his time looking at the dirt. Always the dirt, never much at what grew in it.

Dirt was his income.

Suddenly he felt a stabbing pain in his foot and yelped. A massive thorn had punctured the sole of his medically-approved shoe. They were dress shoes with soles more like athletic sneakers. He had never been all that athletic, and as he'd gotten older and fatter, his knees and hips had started to give him trouble. All this walking really wasn't helping. He carefully pulled the thorn from his sole.

He was dizzy and tired. He lay down next to a rock and passed out.

When he awoke some time later, the sun was almost directly overhead. He started walking again, now with a pronounced limp. His foot was swollen—perhaps the thorn had been poisonous. He remembered getting scratched by some plant once as a child, while working with his grandfather, and the blisters it had raised on his arms.

Freeman decided to head for the highest ground he could find and look around. If there were a road or a house anywhere near by, he should be able to see it from a high spot. He walked for a mile or so towards the nearest ridge, then stumbled and collapsed in a heap. *Can't give up*, he thought. *Only two more years until retirement.*

Wearily he climbed, first on two feet, then on all fours. Eventually he reached the ridge, tongue glued to the inside of his mouth, and his hands and feet throbbing with pain. Slowly he stood. The ridge was scattered with blasted red stones and anemic-looking cacti.

In every direction the land was cracked and rugged, desolate and empty.

He looked up. Vultures were circling.

It was then he realized he was going to die.

✳ ✳ ✳

The Dilbert book would arrive in two days. Jack just had to walk carefully until then. Be friendly, be careful, be competent. No big deal. He walked in the front door of the lab, deliberately thinking positive, whistling a little tune to himself. Angie was on the phone again.

"...and it wasn't chicken pox, of course it wasn't. Cats can't get that. No, it was shingles... cat shingles... He was scabbing up when I..."

Jack slipped through rapidly, breathing a deep sigh of relief when the doors clicked behind him and the familiar plastic-and-chemicals smell of the lab enveloped him. He waved at Raman, who ignored him, then walked back to his station in the lab.

Bill was out of the lab. His 30th anniversary was this month, and he was spending some of his vacation time taking his wife on a cruise. Jack hoped he wouldn't come back with a tropical disease. Cruise ships were hotbeds for that sort of thing. Drinking, dancing, lots of people packed in together, then bam—you caught the plague. Probably a lot like Europe in the Middle Ages, except without the pork lard pies, architecture and monolithic Church.

Jack carefully sifted his first sample of soil and started grinding. His thoughts wandered until he heard the grinder's motor begin to strain. He realized he was over-grinding the sample and stopped the machine. It wouldn't do to have another incident before Dilbert arrived to sew things up. No slipping up, no making waves.

Jack decided it was time to be really nice to Raman today. He walked to the accessions desk where Raman sat, typing away. Jack slapped him on the back.

"Hi Raman," he said. "Nice to see you. Just wanted to say I'm glad we get to work together. Really am."

Raman grunted sullenly.

"How has your day been?" Jack pressed on.

Raman looked up at him. "Do you really want to know?"

Jack decided he should say he did, so he said, "I do."

"Today has been a strange day for me," Raman said. "You know, Jack, you do not seem to worry about very much, but I do."

"Oh?" Jack said. "Like what?"

Raman stopped typing and looked him in the eye. "Are you afraid of death?"

"Me? No," Jack chuckled, "I have fire insurance, as the pastor says."

Raman rolled his eyes and continued. "I ask you because people die all the time. Sometimes in very strange ways.

"That's true."

"And you could die right now."

"Are you going to kill me, Raman?" Jack said.

"No, I am just making the point that you could die. There are many ways for you to die. Heart failure, food poisoning, a blood clot in the brain. A plane could fall down from the sky and crash through the roof. A freak accident, people would say."

Jack glanced up at the somewhat cobwebby ceiling. It remained reassuringly intact and unpunctured by airliners. "The chances of dying that way must be pretty low, though."

"Yes, the chances would be," Raman said. "But they would not be outside the realm of possibility. People die because of improbable events all of the time. For instance, this morning I was in my truck. You know of my truck, right?"

"Right," said Jack. He knew all about the huge new lifted F-250 Raman's parents had bought him. Not nearly as awesome as Jack's own car, of course. But no car was.

"It is a very nice truck," Raman said. "A very strong truck. It has a solid frame, and it is raised upon a lifted suspension, because my parents want me to be safe."

"And the tinted windows, fender flares, and spinning rims?"

"They are to show off my status, Jack."

Jack had nothing to say to that, so Raman continued.

"I was driving in my truck to work this morning, and I drove over the ramp on the interstate. As I neared the top and looked down at the cars crossing far below, I began to think, 'What if this bridge fails underneath me now. It might. Or a reckless driver may run into me right at this spot and drive me over the concrete edge.' Even a very nice truck cannot save you from a fall like that."

"That's true."

"As I was having this thought, I noticed a concrete truck approaching from the opposite direction. He was headed right toward me, half in his lane and half in mine. It was as if I had called my thought into reality. I slammed my foot on the brake, and the truck continued coming, but at last the driver saw me and jerked back into his lane."

Jack let out his breath. "Yikes, man. They should have divided the lane over the bridge. I don't know why they didn't do that."

"Because the probabilities are low. And perhaps because they sold the project to the lowest bidder. But still, it may be that I caused this to happen by thinking about it."

Jack nodded. "I did that once."

"You caused a concrete truck almost to hit you?"

"No, made something happen by thinking about it. I was up in a tree. We had this kite when I was a kid. It looked like a bat with red eyes. Flew really nicely. But it got stuck in a tree, so I climbed up to get it. It was very high and way out where the branches were thin. I edged farther and farther out on one branch until I could almost reach it. The tree was swaying, and I was swaying with it. But my focus was on the kite. Just as I was about to grab it, I thought, 'What if this branch snaps?'"

"And it snapped and you fell?"

"No, I got the kite and climbed back down. But a week later the tree fell over in a storm. And I think the branch snapped then."

"That is not a very good story, Jack."

Jack shrugged.

Raman pointed at the screen on his computer.

"The reason I have shared all this talk is because one of my professors has recently died."

"I'm sorry, Raman."

"I was not actually that close to him, but we had eaten curry together once."

"He was an old guy?" Jack asked.

"No," Raman replied. "In his early fifties, I think."

"How did he die?"

"He fell into a lava tube."

"And burned up?"

"No. It was an old lava tube. A rocky formation like a tunnel. He died from the fall. And drowning."

"Scenic way to die."

Raman glared, then continued, "It makes you think."

"Sure," Jack said.

"Why was he more than six thousand miles from home, high on a volcano, on an island in the Pacific? He lived in the state of Georgia. And it is now the middle of a semester."

"Sure. Well, I thought you were saying 'It makes you think' and talking about death. You know, 'But for the grace of God there go I' and all that. Ashes to ashes. Makes you think."

"No."

"But death does make you think, though."

"No. The probabilities make me think. Not death itself. Death happens all the time. But not six thousand miles from your home inside a lava tube."

CHAPTER THREE

The leaf mold mixed into the new bed had darkened the soil nicely and it was ready for planting. Jack rifled through a Ziploc bag of seed packets and pulled out the "Pima Orange" lima beans he'd been dying to try. They were a runner type, so he reminded himself to cut some river cane for stakes before they started sprawling.

As he planted, he heard Pak Choi humming to himself on the other side of the fence. *That guy gardens almost as much as I do*, thought Jack, *and that's saying something.* Jack finished the last little row of beans, then had a thought: *Maybe Pak knows who is on the sphere. One of the faces was Oriental. Someone from Chinese history?*

"Hey Pak," he called over the fence. "I have something weird to show you—don't go anywhere."

Jack went inside and found the sphere behind the toilet again, then brought it out. Pak was standing by the fence, watering can in hand. "Here, catch!" Jack said, tossing the shiny sphere to Pak, who caught it deftly, barely moving his arm as he snatched it from the air. Pak took one look at the sphere and dropped his watering can. It hit the ground with a thunk and a slosh, pouring some unknown and aromatic liquid across the mulch and in slow rivulets under the fence into Jack's yard.

"Jack! Where did you...?"

"Who are they, Pak? Any ideas? Is the white guy Moses, maybe?"

Pak shook his head.

"Aristotle? Abraham? St. Jerome? That Asian guy, Confucius?"

Pak was still shaking his head. "Jack, this, this sphere... it's—"

"Maybe a hipster? One of those Millennials with an ironic beard? Or hey: Rip van Winkle? Old Man Time?"

Pak was pale. "The man on this side is Marx, Jack. Karl Marx."

"The founder of communism? That's out of left field."

"Very far left, Jack."

"So what about the other guy?"

"I believe he is Laozi, Jack."

"Lousy? That's not nice. You probably never even met the guy."

"No," said Pak. "Laozi. The founder of Taoism. The Supreme Old Lord. Where did you get this? Wait! Don't tell me now. Don't say anything. Say nothing at all. Just put it in your pocket, okay? We must talk at some point, but until then, say nothing about this."

"I'm guessing it's not from a vending machine, then?"

Pak put his fingers to his lips and handed the sphere back to Jack. "Say nothing, Jack. Nothing."

Jack shrugged again, considered saying "Nothing" in a deep voice, but decided that would be childish. Pak nodded sharply at him, then disappeared inside. It was getting dark, so Jack did the same.

* * *

"I'm just afraid of them catching on fire, Franklin! I don't think you are seeing the risk here. Fur is highly flammable and there are literally dozens of places where electric current is buried in my walls!"

Jack tiptoed past, holding his breath. He was almost to the door when Angie held up a finger.

I could ignore her finger and run... Jack thought.

"Well I don't care what the chances are, there is still a chance. You're an electrician and you helped build the place. I want you to figure out a solution. Pay you? Ha! There is a house full of innocent creatures in danger and you talk about money? What is wrong with you? Hello? Hello?"

Angie slammed down the receiver.

"MEN!" she huffed, then smiled at Jack. "Present company excluded, of course. I've got a message for you. Someone left a voicemail asking about our soil testing methods. Mr. Hardin is out and Bill is away on his cruise. That leaves you to explain what we do. Would you call him back? He sounded important."

"Can't Raman do it?" Jack asked.

"No. Raman says he's too busy cataloging a big set of samples from that big customer in Iowa. It's you."

Jack nodded, walked to the lab door, and put his hand on the handle. Angie cleared her throat. Jack turned back slowly.

"Cats *can* get into outlets, you know. Some of them have prehensile tails. Mr. Wiggles does. He licks his tail to a slick, wet point. You cannot tell me he is not at risk of a high voltage incident."

Jack sighed. "Angie, wall sockets don't have that high of a voltage inside, actually. Your standard outlet is just 110 volts. And it's AC."

"I don't care how many volts run through my AC, Jack. 110 volts is STILL 110 volts too many to run through one of my babies!"

"Well–"

"No well about it, Jack. Are you REALLY going to stand here and try to downplay the fiery execution of the sweetest, most harmless creatures on the planet? You would probably pull the switch, wouldn't you, Jack? Pull the switch while Franklin poured in more juice at the breaker box, Jack? Wow! I thought better of you! You're going to just stand there and–"

But Jack was no longer standing there.

* * *

Safe again in the sample room, Jack slouched down at the corner desk to call the man who wanted information about their methods. Then he realized Angie hadn't given him the number. *Off the hook*, he thought. He grabbed a sample, took it to his grinder and started sifting it. A moment later, though, the phone on the corner desk lit up. He flipped the grinder off with a sigh and answered.

"Jack, here's the number," said Angie, no longer sounding irritated. He wrote down the digits, then hung up before she could begin harassing him about flaming cats.

Jack picked up the phone again and dialed. It rang three times, then he heard a faraway click and, "Hello. Who is this?"

"Broccoli. Jack Broccoli. From AgriTweak."

"Ah yes," the voice continued in a smooth, unidentifiable accent. "I wish to speak with you about your methods."

"Sure. We do a variety of soil tests. For example, Mehlich III. We also do ammonium acetate. And sometimes–"

The voice cut him off. "And in doing these tests, is it true that you heat the soil in an oven, then grind it in a machine?"

"Yes, that's right. We put the samples in a drying oven, then we grind them finely. Without doing that, we can't get good readings."

"And then," said the voice, "you pour toxic chemicals onto it?"

"Not super toxic," said Jack. "I mean, just whatever we need to break it down properly to get our readings. It's pretty safe."

"Safe!" hissed the voice. "Safe to who? You, human—that is all you think about! You are blind."

"No," said Jack, slowly, "I'm not. I don't think OSHA would allow that."

"Yes, yes, you are blind. Do you allow the denizens of the soil to evacuate before you initiate your pogrom against them?"

"I'm sorry?" Jack said.

"All the life. The intricate web. The entire cultures you destroy with such callous abandon. Another day on the job for you. Another day of genocide!"

"What are you talking about?" Jack said.

"I am talking about your sins. Sins so dark you cannot even see them, for if you did, you would weep for the suffering and destruction you cause. I would say that you are scum, but that would be an insult to the rich and diverse microbial community which makes up what humans call 'scum'."

"Excuse me?" Jack said, astonished.

"You destroy life, you murderous mammal. Drying, grinding, heating—murder. Know this," the voice continued, "the days of your domination will come to an end. Before proceeding, I wished to know and record the speech of your lips condemning yourself, as it is only fair to let the accused present their case before execution."

"Execution?" Jack exclaimed. "Wait, what? Didn't you want a soil test?"

"The ultimate test is upon man. It is the test of his fitness as a species. And many—too many—are like you. You have failed."

The phone clicked. Jack stared at the dead receiver. *That was weird.*

* * *

When Jack got home, he decided he needed a serious workout before doing anything in the garden. His brother Drew had loaded up his laptop with a variety of martial arts videos a few years back and Jack had been training regularly with them ever since. The videos consisted mostly of ripped men and women throwing punches and kicks, interspersed with loud-voiced guys yelling about "leverage" and "situational awareness" and the occasional shout-out to electrolytes. Jack had now learned Jiu-Jitsu, basic boxing, knife and fork throwing, machete fighting, Congolese wrestling and "how to be invisible like a NINJA".

He wasn't sure how helpful his training would be when he got in a real fight, but he was hopeful. Unfortunately, people rarely challenged him to fights. He had grown up in a safe neighborhood and still lived in one. Jack had thought about joining a dojo, but never got around to it. *It's not like I'm ever going to be a serious fighter, having to rely on my lightning reflexes and a threadbare mop to fight my way to safety,* he thought. It was just more fun to exercise with fighting videos than it was to do Pilates or *Buns of Steel.* He occasionally thought about doing *Buns of Steel* just because of the cover on the video but he never, ever told anyone that.

Jack hooked up his laptop to the larger flatscreen in his living room and found his next video. *Filipino Butcher Masters III.* Parts I and II had been hard to follow, as the English subtitles didn't seem to relate to the language the instructors were speaking or anything they did on the screen. From what he could pick up, "Butcher Fighting" was based on ancient culinary traditions, back in a dim, pre-colonial era when various chefs literally fought each other for dominance.

Thus far, Jack had learned to remove an assailant's eye with a quick, jabbing thrust of a special, hand-carved jade soup spoon known as the "sirain ang mata ipatupad". He didn't have the proper spoon, so he was using a plastic spork. There was also a sort of ritual dance that went along with the attack. Jack was already quite good at it. A quick set of steps, a pirouette, then a feint and a thrust with the opposite arm, along with a spin of the wrist and—voila!—no more enemy eyeball. The end of *Filipino Butcher Masters II* demonstrated a double-handed eyeball attack with the "dalawang mata sirain ipatupad", but Jack didn't have anything like that tool either, so he stuck to the single attack. And taking two eyes seemed excessive.

On screen now was a man dressed in a butcher's apron, wielding a small object and looking cautiously from side to side. The view switched to show an orange face looking in the window. With a quick leap, he jumped into the room. He was a carrot man! Though the foam costume was bulky, the carrot man did a series of fast motions with his arms and legs. Ninja motions. The view switched again, revealing sacks of rice and pots behind the carrot man. Another cut, and the butcher was looking right at the viewer, while behind him, up crept the ninja carrot! Closer, closer, closer, then—so fast it was almost imperceptible—the butcher spun around and stabbed the carrot with a pair of salad tongs, apparently known as the "sagradong litsugas", according to the subtitles, which read "Stirke at man spid With sagradong litsugas!"

The butcher held the carrot man in an improbable grip with the sagradong litsugas, while hitting him in the face with the "gulay na isda".

"The gulay na isda is o fish made from the latex sacred hit! Repear motion pupil!"

Jack dutifully repeated the motions being looped on the screen, though he was starting to wonder if this was a serious martial art or an elaborate troll. He had tried to look it up online when he first started training with this series a month or so back, but had found nothing. The part where they showed how to beat up a watermelon monster with a stand mixer had made Jack wonder a bit, but this bit with the carrot man and the rubber fish was stretching his suspension of disbelief. Maybe it was time to drop the series and go back to *Ab Destroyers 5000*. But Jack wasn't a quitter.

His mind wasn't really on the video anymore, though he kept copying the motions and dancing around the living room. He was thinking about his talk with Raman. It was true that death could get you at any time.

Heck, maybe I'll really screw up a soil sample some day and Hardin will kill me.

He thought back to a story he had read earlier in the week. A man wearing some kind of makeshift loincloth had been mauled to death by a tiger at a zoo. *Come to think of it, the loincloth guy had also been a professor of something.*

On Jack's television screen the butcher was now holding a girl by the throat and shaking her. She shot a pair of "pag-inom ng tubo ng kamatayan" from her sleeves and stuck them in the butcher's ears, causing him to fall into a pool of blood on the floor. The scene was repeated again.

"Repeat Take pag-inom ng tubo ng kamatayan fast attacking from hidden cloth!"

Jack was wearing a short sleeved shirt, and he had no bamboo drinking straws handy to shoot from them, so he decided he'd had enough. He was perspiring profusely but felt like taking on an entire gang of thugs in ill-fitting vegetable costumes. These videos got him pumped.

Since it was on his mind, he looked up the story of the guy eaten by a tiger. Dr. Leighton. Interesting—he was a soil science researcher. Jack wondered if he could find Raman's professor as well. He DuckDuck-

Goed "professor lava tube death" and found the story immediately. Also interesting. The guy had been a geologist. Another soil-related death?

And that phone call today—what if...?

Naw. That's crazy.

* * *

After his workout, Jack had done some weeding, then decided to hunt some new seeds on the 'net for his later season garden. He wanted awesome heirloom types and the local joints didn't carry much. He'd gotten lost in the online catalogs and ended up impulse-buying three varieties of dent corn, lemon cucumbers, purple carrots and a stainless-steel spade. He wasn't sure why, but the pictures compelled him.

It was almost midnight now. Even though Jack was fascinated by the soil mineralization PDF he was reading on his phone, his eyelids were drooping. He pushed the sleep button on his phone, then went to the almost dark kitchen. He felt vaguely hungry, so he opened the fridge. Inside was a half-pound of raw bacon, two Celery Stouts, a cabbage and a slightly moldy block of cheddar entombed in greasy plastic wrap.

Perfect.

He took out a stout, the cabbage, and the cheese. He thought about frying the bacon but decided it would take too long. *Should I nuke it? No, it's just not the same.*

He hacked the cabbage in half, then cut one of the halves in half. He scraped the moldy edges from the cheese with the same knife. Grabbing the stout, he popped off the top on the edge of the counter with a swift blow of his fist—and promptly shot fizzing green foam all over the tiles. He sucked at top of the bottle, consuming the still-emerging foam, unwilling to waste any more of the precious stout.

Lunging for the paper towel dispenser on the other side of the counter, he accidentally knocked the three-quarters of a cabbage onto the floor. This was immediately followed by a bottle of Sriracha he had neglected to put away after some previous meal. He had also failed to close the bottle, as was now evidenced by a spurting stream of bright red pepper sauce that skittered across the floor and mingled with the fizzing green puddle of ale.

Jack nearly got angry. This was not how he had envisioned his midnight snack. Grabbing a fistful of paper towels, he knelt down on the floor by the cabinets and began vigorously wiping up the mess. He was startled by a voice coming from no apparent direction.

"Jack—we need to make tea!"

Jack stood up, banging his head on the edge of the counter and simultaneously knocking down both the paper towel roll and the rest of his beer, which shattered magnificently. He spun around, ready to fight, and saw Pak Choi climbing out from the cabinet beneath the sink. Pak whistled lowly, looking at the floor. "Wow, Jack—you are a slob!"

Jack said something unprintable and threw the now-soiled roll of paper towels at Pak, who dodged gracefully and winked. "Tea time, Jack!" he said, pulling a black box from under the sink. It had tubes and a wire extending from it. "Look—I also brought some pantyhose!" he continued, holding up a soiled pair of extra-large hose.

"What in the name of Steve Solomon are you doing in my house?" Jack exploded.

"Shh, Jack. Say nothing. Go get compost."

"Pak, it's midnight. You're in my house at midnight. With pantyhose and—is that an aquarium pump?"

"I said say nothing. Compost, now! And a bucket. And molasses. You have molasses?"

✳ ✳ ✳

Pak carefully packed compost into the pantyhose, then hung it in the bucket of water he'd filled from the rain barrel outside. "Can't use tap. Will kill it!" He plugged in the aquarium pump and coiled its hose down into the bucket of water. Lacking molasses, he had thrown a cup of brown sugar into the water "to feed them", he had explained. The engine's hum was irritatingly loud in the nighttime stillness.

"You've been on Pinterest again, I see," Jack said. He knew his weird neighbor was a Pinterest addict. Personally, he thought Pinterest was for women and girls, not men.

"There is nothing wrong with Pinterest. I built my vermiculture tower from plans on Pinterest site. Works nice, too, though I skipped the stencil of cartoon worm on side. Was not integral to design. Just whimsy."

Jack rubbed his eyes and sighed loudly. "Okay, Pak. You came over here to make compost tea. Why?"

"So we can talk."

"We can talk without a bubbling bucket of microbes in the living room."

"No, Jack, we can't. You have internet connection here right now?"

"Why? You think the microbes will be looking for a hot spot?"

"No. Not thermophilic types. We need to disconnect. Where is phone jack?"

"Over on the wall, there." Jack jerked his thumb towards a mess of lights and wires emerging haphazardly from the back of his desk.

Pak went over and carefully unplugged the connection. "They can hear you through microphone on computer hooked to lines on internet, Jack. See you, too, through built in iPad camera, phone camera, computer webcam."

"The microbes?"

"Jack, don't be dumb. No, *they*. The reason I am making tea. Also may be bugs in here."

"Bugs—like, spy microphones?"

"Perhaps literal bugs."

Jack raised an eyebrow.

"You must know," Pak continued. "Some carefully modified insects are now used by spy agencies and clandestine organizations. Some are robots, some biological. Used as transmitters."

Jack grunted incredulously.

"Bubbler will help hide sound of our talk from all of above," Pak finished.

"Pak, just tell me what this is about!"

Pak steepled his fingers together, leaning forward on the sofa. "First, Jack, I need to know everything about your sphere."

"Church, work, social life?" Jack ventured.

"No. Shiny sphere you found."

Jack nodded. "It was in a soil sample I was grinding. I found an arrowhead in a soil sample once—that was cool—and I've found nails, brass casings, pottery shards, and even an old agate marble, but this thing looks new."

"Yes, it is new. Did anything else strange happen this week?"

Jack shrugged. "Not that I can think of," he said, then he remembered the phone call. "Actually, Pak, I don't know why you're interested in all this stuff, but I did get a weird call today. Guy with a smooth voice, but he sounded foreign. He said he wanted to know about our methods. Then he said I was evil and I was going to be executed."

"This is what I feared, Jack. You are indeed in grave danger," Pak whispered. "Though it may not seem connected as I say it now, you asked why my trip was cancelled. I am going to tell you."

＊ ＊ ＊

Sitting in church the next morning, bleary-eyed, Jack thought over the previous night's conversation. Pak wasn't merely an eccentric neighbor. He claimed to be a practitioner of an ancient form of battle—Mung Fu, a martial art rooted in gardening techniques.

The trip Pak had planned was for his elevation to the 9th Dan. There were to have been weeks of training, followed by sparring and tests until the final initiation. All of the students and masters had arrived at the event, save one. Master Rice, the greatest modern practitioner of Mung

Fu, and the man who was to have overseen Pak's testing for the rank of 9th Dan, had disappeared without a trace. The Mung Fu community believed that a group calling themselves F.A.D.A.M. was responsible.

Pak suspected that the man who Jack had spoken to on the phone was one of them, and that he was dangerous. He promised to meet with Jack again in the future to formulate a plan. Jack hoped he'd get more answers.

"...and many of you have seen these trees," Jack heard the pastor say, perking up at the word *trees*. "There are sycamores growing even here on our church grounds!"

Jack was horrified. This was a major taxonomic error, yet the pastor continued in blissful ignorance. "As you leave this morning, look up. Picture yourself rising above the crowd and looking for a glimpse of the Savior..."

He clenched his fists.   It was well-known that the so-called "sycamores" of North America weren't even slightly related to the tree known in the Holy Land as a sycamore. That was a fig, in fact, pollinated by a wasp. Sure, there was a similarity between their leaves, and this had inspired the common name of the trees which were, in fact, growing in the church yard—but that was it. Jack wondered grimly if he would have to leave this church. It was so hard to find a good congregation, but this was indeed a serious error. How could he consider the Creator when the pastor couldn't even get the Creation correct?

After the sermon concluded, and the final strains of the Doxology faded away, Jack walked out and got in his car, feeling more alone than he had felt since discovering that wide row spacing in traditional farming had nothing to do with tractors and everything to do with availability of rainfall.

There were only crumbs left in the bottom of the bag of *Ocean Octaves!* Jack was hungry, having skipped breakfast to make it to the service on time. He tried to pour the dusty crumbs of seaweed crisps into his mouth while driving but ended up dribbling them all over his dress shirt. Carefully, he picked off and ate each crumb. The paper bag was empty. He raised it to his face and sniffed, and it smelled like it might still have some of the tasty seaweed essences in it.

This is crazy, he thought. *I almost want to eat the bag. I need to quit these things.*

As he drove he looked at the plowed fields on other side of the highway. Perfect rows of good soil. Ancient soil, the kind he tested every day. Minerals, organisms, humus—the stuff of life. Suddenly he realized that he was chewing on the empty bag. Incredulously, he looked at what was left. He'd eaten half of it.

Yeah, I really need to quit.

CHAPTER FOUR

The next morning Jack arrived at the office bright and early. He let himself in, pleased to see he had beaten Angie in for once. He hadn't beaten Raman, however. The man stood in the hallway, hands shaking.

"Jack!" he said.

"Good morning."

"No, Jack, it is not. They are gone. All are gone."

"What are gone, Raman?"

"Everything. Every sample."

"What?" Jack said, not sure he'd heard correctly.

"Soil sample. Every one. Gone."

Jack shook his head. "That makes no sense. Who would take them?"

They walked together into Raman's office. All the samples were indeed gone. Racks and racks—empty!

"Let's check the grinder room," Jack said.

They did. The samples were gone there as well. Even the ones left on the oven rack were gone. It was a soil lab with no soil to be seen.

"We have to call Mr. Hardin, Raman."

Raman nodded.

Jack picked up the phone. The line was dead. Nothing. Jack realized they might be in big trouble.

"Raman, we have to get out of here!"

"Jack, why?"

"Just go. Now! We need to go!"

Jack ran towards the front. Angie had just settled in at her desk.

"Well, Jack, you're here early," she said, batting her eyes at him.

"Angie, we need to go."

"Go? What are you—wait, do you hear something?

A sudden explosion of breaking glass riveted their attention to the front door as a vehicle plowed into the room. The front was hopelessly smashed up and Jack realized it was one of those tiny, tin-can style "smart cars". There was no driver and the interior of the car was packed with containers of liquid. A few had ruptured in the crash and fluid was splashed across the floor. The unmistakable scent of pine reached their noses.

"What is that smell?" Raman yelled.

"Turpentine," Jack said, backing away.

"What's that?" said Angie.

"A volatile and extremely flammable substance extracted from pine resin. Get to the back!" Jack yelled, grabbing Angie by the arm and pushing her in front of him. They slammed through the door into the strangely soil-less soil lab and went for the back crash door that led into the alley. Jack ran into the bar full tilt and came to a painful halt, his wrists jolted brutally as the door resisted his attempt to open it.

"Locked!" he yelled. "It's locked!"

There was a sudden *WHUMP* of combusting turpentine, then the door leading to the reception area started to blacken, and the air rapidly grew hot. Above them, smoke curled from the ceiling panels. The lights went out, leaving them lit on one side by the hellish glow leaking around the door from the fireball consuming the lobby and on the other by the dim daylight coming through the dusty crank windows along the ceiling of the lab.

"We need to get up there!" Angie yelled.

Raman pushed a wheeled desk chair up to the wall and stood on it. Still not high enough. Jack grabbed the edge of a work table and pulled it to the wall. "We can put the chair on the table," he said.

"That's almost certainly not OSHA approved!" Raman gasped, choking on the thick air.

The room darkened with smoke as the roaring flames out front consumed the door and licked their way down the hallway. Acrid burning insulation and chemicals tore into Jack's lungs as he hoisted

"That's almost certainly not OSHA-Approved!"

the chair onto the table. Raman collapsed on the other side, leaving him with Angie, who was screaming something about cats over and over again. The room narrowed and faded to black, the heat scorching Jack's hair. He scrambled onto the table, then attempted to stand on the chair, but instead he slipped off the table to the ground–

–and then there was a screech of metal as the crash doors slammed open. The last thing Jack remembered was strong hands dragging him into the gray daylight.

✳ ✳ ✳

"Don't you dare take those," Jack growled as a trio of massive ropy tentacles jerked the bag from his hands. "Those are mine." But it was too late—the squid rapidly retreated with his prize into the murky depths as Jack surfaced, raging with anger.

A seagull eyed him from a rock just above the one to which he clung, just barely keeping his head above the surf. "You were lucky, Jack," it said in a matter-of-fact voice.

"Lucky?" he spat at the seagull, desperately trying to hold on to the rock. "He stole my *Ocean Octaves!* you flying rat of the coast, you ruiner of picnics, you parasite-ridden thief and defender of thieves!"

"You almost became a crisp yourself" said the seagull. Exhausted, Jack lost his grip and descended beneath the surf.

A little while later, he bubbled to the top again, this time in a white room, lying in a bed. Something obstructed his nose. He put his hands up and felt a tube there. He worried for a moment that the squid had come back, then realized it was an oxygen tube. This was a hospital. It must have been a doctor who had taken his bag of *Ocean Octaves!* He'd pay for that.

"Feeling okay, Jack?" said a familiar voice. Beside the bed sat Pak Choi, dressed in a grey and white jogging suit.

"I thought you were a seagull, Pak," Jack said.

Pak nodded sagely but remained silent.

"Angie? Raman? The fire?" Jack asked.

"They lived, Jack. But Angie's hair is a mess."

Jack tried to sit up, taking a breath through his mouth as he did so. That hurt—badly.

"Smoke inhalation, Jack. I do not believe it is too severe, though," Pak said.

Jack shook his head. "It feels like I inhaled razors. Tell me, Pak, was it F.A.D.–"

Pak put a hand over Jack's mouth. "Silence! Not now. You will be better soon. They will let you out. Then we talk."

Pak stood up, nodded his head at Jack, then started for the door.

"Wait... Pak?"

He turned back.

"They burned the place down. Turpentine in one of those stupid little cars. And the place was already on fire. The doors were locked. And they stole all the soil samples. But somebody opened the doors. Who? Who got us out?"

Pak smiled at him.

Jack nodded. "It was you, then? I figured it was."

Pak raised an eyebrow.

"Yeah, despite how weird you are, I knew you were watching out for me. I trust you," said Jack. And he did.

"Why do you say that?"

Jack stretched his muscles, wishing he could get up and pace, but he made do with cracking his knuckles. "Well, Pak, to put it simply: you can trust gardeners. Some of the few people in this messed up world you can trust. Everyone else is in it for themselves. For their jobs, their status, their petty little plans. Not gardeners, though. They're in it for the love of God's green earth, for growing things, nourishing and bringing forth life from the soil. They're there for roots and shoots and trees lit with the honest gold of the afternoon sunlight, not the fool's gold of the rat race. I learned early not to trust anyone who didn't have a garden."

"It is a character flaw," Pak agreed, "indicative of deeper issues. Much like irregular row spacing."

"Right," said Jack. "If you garden, you're probably okay. If you don't, I don't trust you. Like I said, I learned this a long time ago, Pak. Back in kindergarten this girl Sarah pulled up all my beans. They were doing great. She said she wanted to see the roots. The roots! She murdered them! I could have throttled her."

"Yes, but then you would be in prison."

"You don't go to prison if you kill someone in kindergarten. In fact, it may be the safest time to do so. Now it's too late. She's probably down in the Amazon right now, feeding rare orchids into wood chippers."

"Almost certainly," said Pak. "Thank you for sharing that story of your sad early life with me. I am sorry to hear of your past pain."

Jack shrugged. "It's just life, Pak. Oh, and before you go?"

"Yes, Jack."

"I need something from you. *Ocean Octaves!* Just one bag. No, two. Get me two bags."

* * *

The hospital set Jack free the next morning. Jack decided he would just go back home and crash for a few days, then re-think his life a bit. He called a friend to get a ride home but didn't talk much because his throat and lungs still hurt, and he felt dizzy. His face and arms looked sunburned, but other than that he was in good shape.

He waved goodbye to his friend and walked to the front door. As he felt in his soot-stained pants for the keys, he had a thought. Leaving the door, he walked out to the mailbox. The seeds had arrived. Maybe he could just garden for a bit, then go inside.

Jack walked around back towards the garden beds, tearing open the box as he did, then chucking the cardboard into the compost bin after pulling out a fistful of seed packs. They had thrown in an extra pack. Black hot peppers. They would be fun to try. He hoped they were really spicy. Anything less than Thai hot wasn't going to do it for him.

The weeds were creeping into some of his beds. No sign of the Pima Orange lima beans yet. *Should be any day now*, Jack thought. He looked over at the turnips. The Kiikala bed was really looking great. He spent a few minutes carefully weeding it, but just that little bit of work tired him. It was too warm out, and Jack felt weak, despite his desire to work the soil.

He unlocked the back door and went inside. As he did, he heard the sound of an aquarium bubbler coming from the living room. Cautiously he walked around the corner. There in the middle of the living room floor was a bubbling bucket of brown liquid, and on his battered sofa sat Pak Choi with two other individuals, both Asian.

Pak smiled. "Tea time, Jack."

* * *

"...and it is our belief that your Mr. Hardin is a primary target, though they are after you as well." The speaker was a sharp-featured and almost painfully thin Chinese man with black-rimmed glasses and silver hair. "Burning the lab is the farthest they have yet gone in an attack. Before, we have only seen isolated attacks on individuals, explainable as accidents, though often under very strange circumstances. They are more subtle than you might expect from their radical ideology. I have made a guess that you, Jack, caused them to attack in a fit of rage."

"Me?" Jack said.

"Yes. Your casual description of what they consider mass murder brought down a brutal reprisal."

"The lab? The man on the phone?"

The Chinese man nodded.

"But what about Hardin? He's at the ABA Conference right now. Always goes. Takes his wife, too, usually—makes a week of it."

"ABA?" the severe-looking man queried.

"Agricultural Business Association."

"Ah yes," he said, "forgive me. It has been a long time since I was involved in the nitty-gritty, as you American businessmen might say."

"No forgiveness necessary. Just be happy you don't have to go. You sit through a day of talks about the regulatory environment, then huge chemical companies handing out environmental responsibility awards, followed by endless golf games—it's terrible. Hardin loves it, though. Says it reminds him of his days in the service."

"He is in grave danger, Jack," Pak said. "Perhaps he will come home soon, once he hears about the fire from the authorities. But let's talk about you, first."

"Me?" Jack said, wishing he had some *Ocean Octaves!* then remembering there was an empty bag in the trash. He considered retrieving and then chewing on it, but decided that was too stupid to consider, especially in front of guests. "What do you need me for?"

They had already questioned him about the fire and the strange phone call, then asked to see the chrome sphere. Jack had figured they were doing some investigation of their own and would soon move on. Sure, they were pleasant enough, in a serious way, but Jack had his own plans, and few of them involved sitting around chatting.

The third man spoke up. He was shorter and broad-shouldered, bald on top with a pot belly, though he still appeared to be carrying a good bit of muscle mass.

"Jack, you are a dead man walking."

"I don't think so," Jack said. "They told me the smoke inhalation would heal up."

"No, Jack. You were not supposed to live. Like it or not, you have stumbled into something greater than yourself. You can move forwards or you can die."

"Die?"

"Yes, Jack. You will cease to live. You will cross the Jordan. You will be extinguished. Kaput. Post-vital. At some point, they will finish what they have started."

"You know more than I do," Jack shrugged. "But what about Raman and Angie? Are they safe?"

The man cocked an eyebrow at him. "Did they speak with the smooth-voiced man?"

"No, I don't think so," Jack said.

"Did they say they killed millions on a daily basis?"

"Wait—what? I don't kill millions on a daily basis."

"Yes, Jack, you do. Millions of microbes."

"Microbes? They count those?"

"Yes, they do. Chances are that you were the only target of that attack. You are the one with cytoplasm on your hands. Angela and Raman would have been incidental deaths, but will likely be left alone from here. They will only seek to kill you and Hardin."

Jack exhaled sharply. It hurt and he started coughing. Pak walked to the kitchen and came back with a glass of water.

"Thank you, Pak," Jack wheezed, glad it was water and not compost tea. "Much appreciated."

The balding man continued. "We don't know everything about this organization yet. It's very strange. The group started as a kind of Korean farming co-op with communist overtones, but it later became like a virus and sent agents around the world."

"Hence the Karl Marx face?"

"Yes," the man nodded. "They were attempting to merge the principles of communism with organic farming and Taoism."

"And then they started killing people," Jack said. "Makes sense. Marxists always start killing people."

"Like it or not, you must now either fight or die."

"Wait a minute," Jack said. "You said they were a natural farming co-op? Did they ever publish any books?"

"Yes," the thin man said, "they have published certain volumes on their methods."

"Ah," said Jack, jumping up and going to his bookshelf. He pulled out a thick paperback in a hot pink binding.

"This volume, perhaps? *Farmers Against Digging Agricultural Method, English translation, with Pictures of Famous Fungi and Appendices.*"

Jack put his hand to his face. "Whoa, wait a minute. These guys, they're Korean. Farmers Against Digging—that's F.A.D.A.M.!"

The men nodded. "You learn quickly," said the thick muscular man. "Mr. Choi said you knew much of the world of gardening, but we did not expect you to have their book in your possession."

Jack shrugged. "I collect books on agriculture. I saw this one mentioned in a forum and got the English translation off Amazon. There's a follow-up volume, but I don't think it's been translated yet."

"And did you learn anything useful from this book?" asked the thin man.

"No, not really," said Jack. "I mean, some of it was interesting. The fungi soup was supposed to help increase root growth and deter pests, but I don't think I did it right. You're supposed to use a boiled carrot for the medium, and I used a beet. And I think I waited too long before application, and the good bacteria died. Or maybe it just doesn't work. Really, the whole book struck me as more philosophical than practical. Lots of philosophy and warnings against tilling. As Pak can tell you, I'm a digger, not one of those 'walk lightly' pansies."

The muscular man nodded. "We figured as such. And we need people like this." He took the book from Jack's hands and turned through the pages. "All this material, this research—good work for what it is. A specific agricultural method for a specific place. Yet then something happened and the writers radicalized. They're no longer interested in this method," he thumped the book with his knuckles, "being just one option. It is to be the only method."

He handed the book back to Jack and continued, "We are making you an offer, Jack. Though we do not normally recruit this far afield, you have been vouched for." Jack looked at Pak, who nodded at him. "Your old life is done, whatever decision you make, but we would like you to join us."

Jack looked around the room. He knew nothing of these men or their organization. Yet it was obvious his old life was indeed done, vanished in one mad day of stolen soil samples and greasy turpentine smoke. It might be worth joining, provided it wasn't all going to be meetings. He weighed it in his mind. "Tell me, gentlemen: what do you want me to do? And why would you pick me for your organization?"

The gray-haired man spoke up. "We believe you know about F.O.R.E.S.T., do you not, Jack Broccoli Junior?"

Jack inhaled deeply and nodded. "A little. My father served with them, as did Mr. Hardin. Neither told me much. But then, I lost my dad when I was young, and Hardin doesn't talk about their time in the service."

"We have worked alongside F.O.R.E.S.T. ourselves, though the relationship has not always been an easy one. Generally, we pursue the same aims, though we are not directly linked to a government, as they are."

"So, why do you want me on board?" Jack said.

"Jack, you love gardening," the thin man said. "You have the passion. You are young and know not the depths of danger in which the world of agriculture groans and turns, waiting for redemption, but you know the drive. The force. The vital life of a seed bursting from the earth. This captures your mind."

"That's true, but I don't even know who you are," said Jack. "For all I know, you could be some sort of corporate espionage outfit."

"You are correct," said the man. "We could be. Yet Pak is with us, and you know Pak. Do you think he would be involved with underhanded dealings?"

Jack thought about it. Pak was a decent guy. He was funny and had been generous in the past, sharing seeds and cuttings. He'd even kept an eye on the house once while Jack was out of town. And pulling Jack out of a burning building counted for a lot. But he'd only known Pak since moving into the neighborhood last summer, and he'd never even been inside his house. Now a secretive international gardening spy organization was asking Jack to join based on the character of this admittedly eccentric neighbor.

Jack, you're tired of a boring life, right? You don't have a wife, you don't have children. Instead, you have a Bachelor's degree and a boring job, and you want more. Even if these guys are corporate spies, won't that be more fun than just existing?

Yeah, Jack, Jack said to himself, *that's all well and good until you end up in jail.*

But how can you end up in jail when you haven't even done anything yet? Listen, Jack—the first time they ask you to steal a bag of seeds, you back out. Don't do anything that violates your conscience and you'll be fine.

Jack looked up at the men. *Here goes nothing.*

"All right, I'm in. But I need to know what's going on. I need more than just 'join our organization and by the way, we're not even telling you its name yet.' "

Pak smiled patiently. "This is reasonable, Jack, though pardon us if we take what you might call a 'rain check' and explain later. Normally, we wouldn't even ask a, how might one say it nicely, a 'white devil' like yourself to join. But I put in a good word for you. And if you don't join, you are likely to be killed within the next twenty-four hours."

"When you put it that way, Pak, it sounds both racist and irresistible. Great—but you will have to explain things to me."

Pak nodded, and the balding man turned to him. "We must go. You are in charge of Mr. Broccoli. May fortune be kind." Pak bowed to the men as they stood and walked out.

"White devil, Pak?" Jack said with a smirk. "Seriously?"

Pak stared at him blankly. "Not the time for splitting rabbits, Jack. Do you want to save your boss's life?"

"Yes, Pak. I do. He's the closest thing to a father I have left." Jack took a last look at the hot pink gardening book, shook his head, then put it back on the shelf. "So, Pak—are you going to teach me Mung Fu?"

Pak shook his head. "No time now."

"But that's basically your gig, right? International martial arts organization or something?"

"Not exactly. The practice of Mung Fu is important, yes, but not all of our agents are excellent at it. Some are selected for other skills as well."

"Do you have any women in this group?"

"No," said Pak. "It is a fraternal order, I think you would say."

"Too bad," Jack said. "So what about–"

"Jack, no more time to explain," Pak interrupted. "We have to go. Now!"

"Where?" Jack asked.

"Scottsdale. Right now."

"What do I need to bring with me?"

Pak shrugged. "Nothing serious. Pants would be good. And shirts. And underwear. And–"

"Right, I get it. Thanks, Mom."

"You are welcome," said Pak. "You also should bring a packet of quick-rising yeast."

"A packet of yeast? Why? I don't even have any."

"You can borrow one of mine," Pak said.

"Anything else?"

"No, that should be it. We can get what we need there. We must go now."

CHAPTER FIVE

As was usually the case in this brave new world of aerial transportation, the flight itself was much more pleasant than the trip through the security theater in the airport. Pak and Jack had a row to themselves. Pak sat quietly in his seat during takeoff. After they were well on their way and he still hadn't said anything, Jack couldn't take the suspense any longer.

"Pak?"

"Yes, Jack?"

"I need to know what's going on. What did I join? Who would want to kill my boss? Or me? Over microbes, I mean–"

Pak put his finger to his lips and shook his head. "You talk too much, Jack."

"I don't think we've talked enough, Pak. I need to know."

"I will tell you eventually. Cannot make tea on plane."

"Ah," said Jack. "Right."

"But we can talk about something else if you like." But Jack didn't really want to talk about anything else. Questions were burning in his mind and he had hours to sit and stew on them.

"We could talk about history, Jack."

"History?"

"Yes, wise men of history."

"Sure, like Marcus Aurelius."

"Ah, you know him?"

"Sure. Not well, really," Jack admitted, "but I did read half-way through his book once."

"The *Meditations*."

"Right."

"There is much wisdom in there, but also some which is not as wise."

"Right, like Aesop's Fables."

"You do not think Aesop's Fables is consistently filled with wisdom?" Pak asked.

"Well, some of them are strange."

"Like 'The Dog, the Squirrel and the Peach Tree'?"

Jack frowned. "I don't remember that one."

"No, probably because it is not in the Dover Thrift Edition."

Jack shrugged, "I just don't remember it. How does it go?"

Pak looked up, as if remembering the story, then spoke.

"Once there was a squirrel who climbed into a peach tree filled with delicious peaches. He was enjoying himself when along came a dog, who, unable to climb, said, 'Oh brother squirrel, will you not throw a peach to me?' The squirrel, no friend of dogs by nature, and remembering how the dog had previously eaten his kin, pretended not to hear the dog. Again the dog asked, 'Brother squirrel, will you not throw down a peach?' And still the squirrel ate, disdainful of the hungry dog. The peach tree, awakened by the voice of the dog, felt the squirrel on its limb eating one of its peaches and threw the animal to the ground where the dog snatched it up in one bite. Yet because the squirrel had been swallowing the peaches pits and all, the dog choked and died at the base of the tree, and the peach fed for many long years on their bodies."

Jack frowned. "That cannot be a real story. What would be the moral?"

"When an enemy is hungry and you are stealing, make sure he doesn't bark at you, lest you get eaten."

"That makes sense. That wasn't one of the weird ones I was thinking about, though."

Pak nodded. "There are many. Is there anything else you want to talk about?"

Jack shook his head. Everything he really wanted to talk about, Pak wouldn't.

"Okay, then, Jack. I am going to shut my eyes. You may want to as well. I have a feeling this will be a tough week." He leaned his seat back and closed his eyes. Jack did the same, but he couldn't stop thinking about the fire, his boss, and the strange metal sphere. *What have I gotten myself into?*

They arrived in the late evening and checked into the hotel. Pak said he was going to do reconnaissance, leaving Jack behind to watch television in their room. He flipped on a reality show about pawn shops. There was a guy trying to sell a collection of vintage diapers to the owner, but the owner was more interested in vintage diaper pins. It was really dumb, and at least two of the characters seemed to be mentally retarded. Jack supposed it was good for the mentally retarded to have work, but he didn't think the show portrayed them in the best light. He wished he had something more interesting to watch, then had the good idea of asking Pak about some Mung Fu moves. That would be cool to learn, and unlike Filipino Butcher Masters, he'd likely own the martial implements already. Unless they were strange Chinese gardening tools he didn't know about. In that case he'd have an excuse to buy some new tools for the garden. Win-win.

As he day-dreamed about fighting off a horde of ninjas with a spading fork, Jack suddenly heard a click at the window of the room. Then another, followed by a scratching sound, as if the glass was being cut. Then a piece of glass fell to the carpet, and the window swung open through the curtains.

A man in black stood in the room with him—and Pak was nowhere to be found.

* * *

Pak skulked through the parking lot, noting the high percentage of rental cars, the high percentage of John Deere stickers, and that there was only a 1% overlap between the two categories. The one percent was composed of a single vehicle—an obviously rented SUV— the back windshield of which sported a "What's Yellow and Green and Mean All Over?" decal. Pak wondered if the driver intended on removing the sticker before returning the car. *Perhaps the man owns the rental company?* This was not likely, he thought, as the overlap between owners of rental car companies and attendees of agricultural conventions was almost certainly lower than the overlap between John Deere stickers and rental cars. *Stay focused*, Pak told himself.

He noticed a man smoking a cigarette at the other end of the lot. The man's face was down and he appeared to be waiting for someone. *Or 'casing the joint'?* Pak thought. *American slang is fun.* As he casually strolled towards the smoking man, he made a mental note to use more slang. The man might be Korean, but Pak couldn't tell for sure. His face was turned away.

Pak decided to take a direct approach. He walked right up behind the man, as silently as possible. "Good evening!" he said in a loud voice.

The man spun around suddenly, letting the cigarette fall and dropping into a defensive crouch. Pak instinctually snapped up his own guard, then realized the man he faced was not Korean. He was Chinese. Not only that, he was an ally—an agent Pak only knew as 10-10-10.

"Pak," the agent said, pulling himself up and giving his fellow agent a slight bow. "I thought you might be here. However, we are not alone. The Koreans are here as well."

"I thought as much," said Pak.

The man took another cigarette, offering one to Pak, who declined. "I have heard of your friend and the fire."

Pak nodded and the man continued.

"Is he fine?"

"Yes," said Pak, "he is fine. He's here."

"Here?" 10-10-10 raised an eyebrow.

Pak nodded again. "Yes, for what better way to strengthen a man than to place him in the forge?"

"This forge may be too hot for him," 10-10-10 said quietly. "There is still no sign of Master Rice."

"Let us hope he is gone for reasons of his own and not due to the schemes of enemies," Pak said.

The agent nodded. They stood there in the chilly evening air, watching the smoke of 10-10-10's cigarette rose in lazy curls, until the sound of breaking glass and a yell smashed their reverie.

✳ ✳ ✳

The man in black was the same size as Jack, but he had a defensive stance, which made Jack wonder if he was overmatched. *Maybe he just came to take the TV.* The man said something through his mask to Jack in badly accented English. It sounded like "Ukom wis mao."

"I'm not sure what you said," Jack replied as his eyes darted around the room, looking for something he could use as a weapon. "Do you want to take the TV?" The man shook his head and took a step towards Jack.

"UKOMWISMEAOW!" he commanded.

"Yukon whiz meow?"

The man ripped off his mask and scowled at Jack. *He must be Korean*, Jack thought, though to his undiscriminating eye he might also be Japanese, Laotian, Cambodian, Taiwanese, Vietnamese, Tibetan, Thai, Indonesian, Chinese, Filipino, Pacific Islander or Cherokee.

"You come. With me. Now!"

"Out the window?" Jack said incredulously.

"No. Out door!" the man snapped, stepping forward and snatching at Jack's arm.

Jack didn't even think about it. He jerked away from the man's outstretched arm and swung his right fist in a big arc towards the man's face—but the man's face wasn't there! Jack lost his balance as the man ducked underneath him into his midsection. Instead of falling on his back, though, he fell painfully on his side, grabbing at the man as he fell. The guy was strong but so was Jack. They rolled on the floor, grappling at each other without luck.

Then a voice came into Jack's mind. A booming, steroid-addled male voice.

EVERYTHING IS A WEAPON.

With a lucky clutch, Jack grabbed the phone cord and yanked the phone off the cheap hotel desk. It fell on the man's face, tangling him up just enough for Jack to kick free and stand up, but the man was right behind him. He heard the voice again.

EVERYTHING!

Jack nodded and grabbed at the carpet at the end of the room. His assailant stared at him in confusion. With a yank, Jack pulled the carpet up and snatched a wad of padding from beneath it, balling it up in his fist.

"Take THIS!" he yelled, throwing the padding at the man. The foam had absolutely no effect.

"I thought you said everything was a weapon," Jack yelled at the voice in his head.

THE TACK STRIP MIGHT HAVE BEEN A BETTER CHOICE.

Jack glanced at the mangled edge of the carpet, then the probable Korean was on him, kicking and battering him about the head. He tried to ward off the blows, screaming incoherent kung-fu phrases at the invader as he did so. In the midst of a particularly good scream, his mouth was suddenly stuffed with padding. *Tricky!* Jack thought, as he gagged and spit. With a lucky strike, Jack brought his knee up violently into the man's gut, breaking the onslaught of blows.

THINK DEFENSIVELY.

He scrambled away, pulling the room's cheap pink and turquoise Southwestern print love seat away from the wall and positioning it between them. He crouched in the corner behind it. The potential Korean was back on his feet. Jack suddenly wondered why the man didn't have a weapon.

Wouldn't it have been easier to bonk me on the head with something or take me out at gunpoint? Did he not expect I would be here? But then, why did he tell me to come with him?

Jack had no time for further thought, as the presumptive Korean lunged forwards and snatched the love seat up into the air. The guy was stronger than he looked. With a powerful swing of muscled arms, he brought the love seat down on Jack.

There wasn't even time to think, yet some part of Jack's mind was ready. He grabbed the cheap lamp off the bedside table and placed it on the floor, crouching down further as he did so. The blow of the love seat was arrested by the thick, cactus-shaped porcelain. Jack yanked one of the wooden legs of the love seat off with a jerk, then stood and flung it with all his might at the perhaps Korean.

To his complete surprise, the leg not only hit his man, *it went right through his chest*. Jack actually heard the sound of the man's lungs exploding. When he was a kid he had been given a shiny silver balloon for his birthday one year. Drew had sat on it, making it decompress with a whoosh of expended helium. Jack had hated that sound ever since—until now. Now it sounded like victory.

Clutching at his chest, the man windmilled backwards and out the window, shattering most of what was left of the glass. Jack yelled in triumph and pumped his fist, then realized he was now liable for murder.

And how in the world would he explain this to room service?

* * *

Pak and Agent 10-10-10 raced towards the source of the sounds—it was around the side of the building from where they were, back toward Pak's room. Thus far, no one else seemed to have noticed. *Wait*, he thought, looking up. *There is a broken window just about where our room is!* 10-10-10 was focused on the ground. There, in the bushes, lay a dead man. A Korean, his chest destroyed.

"Hey!" came a voice from above. They both looked up. It was Jack. "What are we going to do about that guy?" Jack said, trying to keep his voice down.

Pak and 10-10-10 looked at each other.

"Jack is right—we need to get rid of this man or the whole place will be filled with police," Pak said.

10-10-10 nodded and took off his jacket and hat, placing them on the dead man, then hoisting the body up by the arms. He was unable to do it alone, so Pak assisted. "We pretend he is drunk. Like Hollywood movie, we walk him between us, with ball cap down over face, then dump him in my car."

Pak nodded and they half walked, half dragged the man to 10-10-10's vehicle, then stuffed him in the passenger seat, positioning him as if he were sleeping. 10-10-10 got into the driver's side and started the car.

"I will take care of this problem, Pak—you take care of your friend."

"Are you sure, 10-10-10?"

"Yes, do not worry about me. I can now use the HOV lane all I like."

Pak nodded, then jogged back across the parking lot. Jack looked down from the window and waved at him. Pak shook his head and yelled up, as quietly as he could yell.

"Shut the curtains, Jack—get out of window. I am coming up."

Jack gave him a thumbs-up, then the window went dark.

Though Pak didn't feel comfortable cutting his reconnaissance short, it was obvious in retrospect that he should have stayed with Jack. *If we could have captured that man instead of killing him*—but how had Jack killed him? That was impressive. Had Jack found a gun? Had the man fallen onto something?

He reached their room and knocked softly at the door, then opened it with his keycard. Jack sat on a strangely uneven love seat in the midst of a mess. Shards of ceramic, wads of foam... a phone cord?

"Did I tell you before you are a slob, Jack?"

Jack nodded, grinning.

"Why are you grinning, Jack?"

"It worked," he said. "It worked. My training. I beat that guy good."

"You did indeed," said Pak. "You have punched a hole through his chest."

"Yeah," Jack frowned. "I'm not exactly sure how I did that."

"You are not sure? A very nasty wound to be unsure about. Maybe he fell on cactus lamp?" Pak said, gesturing to the broken light fixture.

"Nope," said Jack.

"What about this?" Pak said, picking up the telephone.

"No again," Jack said.

"Or this?" Pak said, waving a complimentary mint in the air.

"No, it wasn't that," Jack said, getting up and looking around, then finally picking up a wooden cylinder off the floor. "It was this." He handed it to Pak. It was sticky with blood. At one end was a broken metal bolt.

"This is the leg to a piece of furniture, Jack? The love seat?"

Jack nodded, sitting back down on the uneven seat.

"Did you hammer it through his chest by using the lamp, perhaps?" Pak asked, eyeing the partially splintered leg.

"No," said Jack. "I just threw it through him."

"You threw it through him?" Pak's eyes widened. "How could you?"

Jack shrugged. "I'm not sure. I really have no idea. But man, that throw felt good."

"Probably not to him," said Pak.

"No, I guess not. But he was probably distracted from the initial pain by falling out the window."

Pak sighed. "Well, I suppose we had better clean up a bit."

Jack nodded, then paused. "Wait, Pak—you think I'll get arrested for killing that guy?"

"No," Pak said. "We have already taken care of it."

"Your friend?"

"Yes. He is your friend too. In this organization, there are many you do not know who are covering for you. Though I recommend being more quiet next time you send a Korean out the window."

"So he was Korean then. I knew it." Jack stood and walked over to Pak and leaned against the wall, "Now how about you tell me what's going on? What have I gotten myself into here?"

"Okay," said Pak, "I will tell you."

＊＊＊

The nights were pleasantly chilly in Arizona, Hardin was pleased to note. Not like nights in Virginia at this time of year. He had heard some weird noises last night, though. He wondered about the local crime rate. Perhaps someone just had their TV cranked up too loudly.

Arizona always reminded him of Mars. As a boy he had devoured Bradbury's *The Martian Chronicles*, and he could picture silver spaceships and crumbling alien ruins amidst the tumbled rocks of the desert.

Ah, fantasy. No time for that nonsense anymore. He was here for business.

Yet he had a lot on his mind now. A fire had broken out at his shop, and the police suspected arson. That seemed quite improbable to him, but whatever the case, he had insurance. He had been glad to hear that none of his employees were seriously hurt, though there was always the possibility one of them would sue. Oh well, again—that's what insurance was for. *This is really going to kill our bottom line this year, though.*

He'd spoken with Angie and Raman, but Bill was on vacation, and Jack wasn't picking up. Poor kid had apparently spent the night in the hospital for smoke inhalation. *Maybe I was too hard on him before I left,* Hardin thought. *He's really a good guy. He's going places someday if he stays on track. But no sense in coddling him. Jack Sr. wouldn't have put up with foolishness, and my job is to fill that gap. Overall, though— despite his poor vending machine record—he's solid. Good thing he came through the fire okay.*

When Hardin had first heard about the fire, he'd almost given up on the convention and raced home, but then he reconsidered. He needed to make big connections here, even if they couldn't make him money for a few months. This was where the deals were made. A burned building could wait. Unfortunately, his wife had taken the news harder than he had. She was really concerned about their future. What she didn't know was that Hardin had assets stacked away she'd never dreamed about. He did some calculations in his head on what it would take to get the shop up and running again. He could make a deal with a friendly competitor to take their samples for a time, get a new place rented, assess the damage—he could do it. It would be hard, but it would all work out.

He pulled back the curtains so he could see the desert from the huge picture window of his suite. Behind him, he heard his wife turn over in bed with a moan. She wasn't the early riser he was. No matter, though, he loved her despite that. She was a good sounding board and also had a memory for names and places that had proven quite useful in the past. And she was just plain cute.

There was a knock at the door. He threw on a robe and answered it. In the hallway stood an Asian man, dressed nicely. "Laundry service, sir?"

Hardin shook his head. "No, thank you."

"You are Mr. Hardin, correct?"

"Yes, that's right."

"Okay, thank you sir. Very good sir." The man bowed and left.

Hardin looked at his watch. *Rather early for a laundry call*, he thought, then dismissed the interruption. He looked at his wife lying on the bed, her long gray and brown hair flowing across two pillows. Her mouth was open and she was snoring slightly. Carefully, Hardin leaned in and kissed her. She frowned and pulled the covers over her head. He patted her rump, then went for the shower.

Just before he stepped in, there was another knock at the door. With a grimace, he wrapped a towel around himself and answered it. A different Asian man stood in the hallway.

"Mr. Hardin?"

"Yes?"

"Laundry service. Do you have any items that need washing or pressing?"

Hardin rolled his eyes. "Listen, buddy, are you guys having some coordination issues around here? Laundry service already came about five minutes ago—the guy just knocked on my door. And it's early. Very early. Do your clients not normally sleep?"

The Asian man looked at him with pursed lips. "I am sorry sir. It must have been a mistake. My apologies."

Hardin waved a hand at him. "No problem. Goodbye." He shut the door, then headed back to get his shower.

* * *

"He's here, Jack," Pak reported. "Sixth floor. 606. In his room."

Jack woke at Pak's voice and tried to jump out of bed, then realized he was sore all over. He put his hand to his face and felt a Band-Aid there.

What in the world? Then he remembered the night before. Had he dreamed about throwing that leg? He looked at the love seat. Nope, not a dream. He had another thought: should he consider joining a baseball team? He shook his head. *No, you're an international spy of secrecy now.*

"What did you say Pak?"

"Hardin is here, Jack," Pak repeated. "Room 606."

"Hmm, no phosphorus," Jack mumbled. "Thanks, Pak." He looked at his friend. "You're dressed nicely," Jack said, getting up carefully.

"Laundry service."

"They came by already?"

"No, Jack. I was pretending to be laundry service. Possibly not a good ruse, as laundry service had already come this morning."

"At this hour?" Jack said.

"I suppose so," said Pak. "He said they had come just before me."

"Pak, what if–"

The two of them looked at each other.

"You are right Jack! We need to run!"

Last night's conversation flooded back into Jack's mind. The world of agriculture was a much more dangerous place than he had ever realized. For some people, gardening wasn't just a hobby. And farming wasn't just a way to—often literally—bring home the bacon. Behind the rows of corn and the raised beds lurked dark and mysterious forces. There were transnational organizations, some who hoped to control the entire food supply—and man himself—and others who fought against the system. There were proletarian terror cells, violent cults, and ancient and powerful families whose farm holdings stretched back into ancient history. There were scientists attempting to create superfoods with potentially dangerous genetic modification, and activists who hoped to end GMO technology by any means necessary. There were secretive New Age groups who planted only on ley lines and transagriculturalists who were inserting RFID chips and electromagnets into crops.

The allegiances between interests and powers were traced on shifting sand—and in the middle was Pak's organization. Founded in the Qing Dynasty shortly before the Opium War, it had gone from being an organization chartered by the government to an entity unto itself. Pak was a high-level agent, he had revealed. When he wasn't working online for an import company owned by his family, he was fighting directly against the forces of evil.

Jack was only the second non-Chinese individual to be allowed in, Pak had said, and that decision had been made by the local chapter, not by the head of the organization. Pak was afraid that once the old-guard heard of the decision, Jack would be ejected. *So don't screw up, Jack. Just follow my lead. You must earn respect.*

And that's what I'll do, thought Jack as he pulled on the jeans he had been wearing yesterday and stumbled around trying to find a shirt. In a moment, both of them were racing down the hall and up the stairs to the sixth floor. They reached it and Pak held up a warning hand. "Stay back, Jack—if Hardin is here he might fire you."

"Naw, Pak, why would he do that? He'll probably praise me for showing up at the convention after the fire."

Pak shook his head. "No, Jack, I am making excuse. Really, I want to do this myself. Do as I say if you want to stay on this team."

"Fine, Pak. I'll hide behind the palms."

Pak went to the door as Jack crouched behind a pair of palms in a large, ornate pot. One of them had three different colors of bubblegum stuck to the back of the trunk. The other was gum-free. Jack wondered if some palms might emit a pheromone that attracted slobs. *What is the fertilizing potential of chicle?* he thought. *Is gum even made of chicle anymore?*

The door had opened, and Pak was speaking with someone who sounded irritated. Pak bowed slightly and the door slammed shut. He walked over to the palms as Jack stood up.

"So, Pak?" Jack said, leaning against one of the trees.

"Hardin is still there. He was angered that laundry service had returned yet again. He is safe for now, I would say."

Jack nodded, then realized his hand was stuck to the palm. "Pak, do you think it could be chewing gum itself that emits attractant pheromones?"

"Yes, quite possible, Jack. Or you could simply be a klutz."

"Yeah, also possible," Jack said, wiping his hand on the inside of the cuff of his jeans. The gum didn't come off all the way, and it was irritating. He wished he had some turpentine, then remembered his last encounter with the volatile fluid and shuddered involuntarily.

The elevator down the hall hissed open. Pak jumped behind the palms and gestured for Jack to do the same. Out of the elevator sauntered a woman in a swimsuit, with wet hair and a towel over her shoulder. She was in her mid-twenties, lean and fit with good curves, hair a rich chestnut brown hanging over her finely shaped face. Her legs were toned and reached all the way to the floor. She had earbuds in her ears and eyes as blue as the Montana sky in July.

She walked right past Hardin's room to where Jack and Pak crouched behind the potted palms. She stopped and looked at them, pulling the earbuds out with a frown.

"Uh, you guys lost?"

Jack shook his head.

"You have a Band-Aid on your face."

Jack nodded.

"So, if you're not lost... what *are* you doing?" she said, popping her gum.

"We're with the S.P.C.P., doing a routine check," Jack said, thinking quickly.

Pak glanced at Jack, then nodded to the woman. "Right, what my friend said. Yes. We are with the Special People Crouching People."

She rolled her eyes. "Whatever floats your boat." Then she kept walking.

Jack elbowed Pak in the ribs. "What the heck was that? The 'Special People Crouching People?'"

"You had a better idea?"

"Uh, yeah. SPCP. The 'Society for the Prevention of Cruelty to Palms.'"

"That's just crazy, Jack," Pak muttered.

The elevator swished open again, and they both hit the ground simultaneously. Three men stepped out. "Sri Lankan?" asked Jack in a whisper.

Pak shook his head. "No. Korean."

The Koreans turned and walked closer. All were wearing suits. One was bulkier than the other two, but they were all fit. They stopped in front of Room 606 and knocked. Out came a muffled voice, loud enough for Jack and Pak to hear. "If this is laundry service, I give up! Just take everything!"

The Koreans looked at each other. "No, not laundry service, Mr. Hardin," one said after a moment. Hardin opened the door. The Korean said something to him, Hardin said something back, there was a handshake, then the door shut again.

The Koreans weren't leaving.

"They're waiting for him to come out, Pak," Jack whispered. Pak nodded.

A moment later, Hardin did come out, wearing his suit. The men laughed and conversed with him as they got onto the elevator. With a swish, they were gone.

"I think those guys are the bad guys, Jack," said Pak.

"Yeah, I think so too."

"So we should go get them."

"Agreed."

They raced for the stairs.

CHAPTER SIX

Though it was unconventional to be greeted in the early morning by other attendees insistent on buying a fellow breakfast, Hardin accepted it as part of the general festival atmosphere of the ABA. There's a light-hearted camaraderie between business owners, regulatory officials, vendors, salesmen and farmers. In between the mind-numbingly boring presentations, that is.

All part of the game, Hardin thought, as he got into a black smart car with the trio of Koreans. *I have plenty of time in the day, and if these men are serious about their soil sampling needs, it will pay for the week many times over.*

Conversation in the car was thin over the fifteen minutes it took to reach their breakfast destination. Hardin sat in the passenger side of the vehicle and watched Scottsdale pass by. It was incredible how vibrantly green the grass was in some yards. He saw a house with an orange tree out front, the grass beneath like a lush emerald carpet. The next house, however, had a square of tastefully laid out gravel, rocks and cactus, enclosed with a block wall. He wondered how much water it took to maintain the lawns here. It was obvious that little grew naturally, save scrappy succulents and brush able to maintain a miserly hold on any moisture from above. The boulders and cacti method seemed like a good bet for the budget conscious.

As he mused upon grasses and irrigation, the car pulled into the parking lot of a small Korean restaurant. The sign out front read "CLOSED", but the driver got out and walked to the door anyway. He rapped twice on the glass, and a small hand waved through the curtains. A moment later, a woman opened the door to let them inside.

It was a nice-looking little place, decorated in a subdued rectangular and square motif with red and black accents. Overhead hung woven lamps of bamboo. They sat at a table towards the back. Hardin noticed that the woman relocked the front door after they entered.

She walked over and bowed to the men, then handed them menus without a word. Hardin looked at his. Nothing on it was in English. He looked up at the others, but they were all studying their menus. Finally, he caught the eye of the driver.

"I'm sorry, but I can't read this—can you help?"

"Ah yes," said all the men simultaneously. "I will order for you. No need to worry."

That was weird, Hardin thought. "Do they have coffee here?"

"I will check when our waitress returns," the driver said.

In a few moments, she did. One of the other men ordered in Korean, nodding at Hardin at one point. The woman nodded back, then took the menus and left.

Well, this is certainly shaping up to be an interesting day.

* * *

Jack watched the small black car pull away from the hotel. Pak was already at the wheel of his rental car, and Jack tumbled in on the other side as Pak snapped it into drive. The car was a few-years-old white Ford Fiesta that smelled slightly of cheap cigarettes barely covered by chemical air freshener, but it was good enough to chase a Smart car. Pak followed it from a distance, trying not to be too obvious.

"Pak, this is crazy," exclaimed Jack. "Those guys—they're from the international cartel of crazy Koreans, right? I mean, they're taking my boss somewhere to kill him, right? And we're following behind them, just like a movie."

Pak nodded.

"Last night was exciting," Jack whistled, "but this is awesome."

Jack looked out the window at a perfect green lawn with an orange tree in the center, next to a xeriscaped plot of ground. *I wonder if*

Hardin notices these details, he thought. *I mean, imagine the cost of keeping up a lawn like that. Probably never even enters the guy's mind.* Then he rebuked himself for being uncharitable. Hardin had always taken care of Jack after his father disappeared. *Who cares how Hardin feels about the price of irrigation? He's one of my people, and I'm going to take care of him. Nobody's dropping my boss into a lava tube.* He paused for a moment, looking out the window for volcanic structures. *Do they even have lava tubes in Arizona? No, probably not. Maybe they'll hang him on a cactus. Or throw him in a pit of gila monsters.*

While Jack was imagining being chewed to death by gila monsters, Pak drove right past the smart car. It was parked in front of a little restaurant. Jack read "Korea Sun" on the sign as they passed.

"Pak, they're there. Why are you still driving?"

"If we stop here, they will see us. We cannot simply walk in through the front door."

"Good point," said Jack, realizing just how green he was at the spy business.

Pak continued down the block, then pulled around the corner and parked in an alley next to a dumpster and the rotting remains of a mattress. They jumped out of the car, but not before Pak grabbed a well-worn transplanting trowel from beneath his seat. Jack noticed and wondered if Pak was planning to do some guerrilla gardening. Pak motioned for Jack to follow him up the alley.

"If I am correct, we will find the back of the restaurant here. Then we can try to get in."

"How will you know what building it is, Pak?"

"By the dumpster."

"I see," Jack said, though he didn't.

As they walked, Pak spoke again. "Jack, did you ever go dumpster diving?"

Jack nodded. "Sure I did," Jack said. "I used to dumpster dive in college. I got a toaster once. And a bike. Two flat tires—just needed air. I also get fuel for my ride sometimes, gathering the used cooking oil. You need to make a deal with the restaurants for that, though."

"Yes, much waste can be reclaimed. I assumed, however, that you might have gone dumpster diving for food."

"Food?" Jack said, with a disgusted look.

"Yes, food. Many people do. I assumed you might have tried it."

'Of course not," Jack said. "Not officially. Though, hypothetically, if I were a starving college student I might look for expired chips or something."

"Ah, this is the place." Pak pointed to a green enclosed dumpster which smelled of fish guts. "Restaurant dumpsters are easy to spot. A properly trained agent can tell the ethnicity of an establishment by the smell of its dumpsters."

Serious spy stuff, Jack thought.

"Stay here, Jack," Pak continued. "I am going to get inside. You stay out of sight of the door, okay?"

Jack nodded, heart now racing. *What if guys with guns come out the back? Or switchblades? Koreans probably carry switchblades.* He wondered if he could evangelize them Pat Boone style before they carved him up. *Or what if I carve them up?* he thought. After last night's fight, that didn't seem as unlikely—yet he couldn't count on that kind of bizarre luck again. *It had probably just been adrenaline.*

Pak pulled a ring with half a dozen keys from his pocket and tried them until he found one that fit the lock on the metal door at the back of the Korean Sun. He pulled it out a fraction of an inch, then bumped the key with the palm of his other hand while twisting. The lock clicked, and the key turned. Pak opened the door and slipped inside, giving Jack a quick thumbs up. The door shut, and Jack was alone with his racing heart and the stench of rotting food.

✳ ✳ ✳

Inside, Pak found himself in a utility room connected to the kitchen. He hovered by the door for a moment, afraid he might have been heard—until the clatter of pans and the bubbling of a boiling pot assured him that his chances of detection via auditory cues was less than likely. He crept closer to the back door of the kitchen, crouching low on the white tile floor.

He saw the front door of the kitchen open and a woman walk through and speak in low tones to the cook. The cook, a burly man with a scar across his forehead, nodded quickly to the woman, then went to the fridge to start gathering raw materials for a meal. As he did, the woman opened a jar of instant coffee. It was obviously old, evidenced by how she whacked it on the counter a few times and then started carving into its contents with a knife. She managed to scrape a teaspoon of crystals out and put them in a mug, which she then filled with water from a steaming teapot. She placed the mug of coffee on a tray along with a second teapot—presumably filled with tea—and various mugs and utensils, then headed out the door of the kitchen.

Meanwhile the cook was busy preparing seaweed and rice with sliced ham and pickles, bowls of kimchi, eggs, and various other dishes and condiments Pak did not recognize.

The cook expertly arranged multiple dishes of food into groupings on four trays, then reached into a cabinet beneath the counter and pulled out a knapsack. He rooted around inside it, then removed a jar. Carefully, he unscrewed the lid and took out a pinch of powder, then dusted it over multiple dishes on one of the trays. The cook then cut one perfect slice from a carrot and placed it on one of the bowls laying on the tray he had just doctored. None of the other dishes received a slice of carrot.

Poison! thought Pak. From the other accounts he had read, it seemed likely the previous victims had been drugged, at the least. *I've got to warn Hardin—or get that tray*, he thought.

The cook washed his hands carefully, then toweled them off. He was going for the door. In a moment he would call the waitress and this food would be headed for Hardin's unsuspecting stomach!

Pak meowed softly.

The cook turned around and frowned, squinting towards the dark utility room. Pak waited a moment and meowed again. The man grabbed a cleaver from the counter and crept softly toward the door. *That I did not expect*, Pak thought.

The cook came closer, stepping slowly into the room as Pak pressed himself against the wall. As the man walked past him, Pak lashed out with his trowel, landing a rapid jab to the back of his head, knocking him cold. The blade fell to the ground with an awful clatter, but Pak didn't hesitate—he raced into the kitchen and grabbed the tray of poisoned food, then ran back into the utility room, just in time.

The waitress came through the front entrance of the kitchen, looked down at the trays, and noticed one was missing. She looked around for the cook with a puzzled expression before walking back out. *Hopefully she just assumes he's left for a moment and hasn't finished the fourth tray yet*, Pak thought. The cook began to groan. Pak gently kicked him in the forehead and he stopped.

Tray still in hand, Pak slipped the back door open and looked for Jack but didn't see him. "Jack!" he hissed. A second later, Jack appeared, and Pak whispered "Take this," as he handed him the plate. Jack took it, then Pak went back inside, silently closing the door behind him.

The waitress was not back yet. Pak slipped into the kitchen and quickly prepared another tray of food, taking small portions of the dishes from the other three until he had assembled a good-looking fourth meal. He carefully took one slice from a carrot and placed it on the new tray. *Perfect*, he thought as he slipped back into the utility room.

It was not a moment too soon: the waitress opened the door, saw the finished spread of food, and looked around for the cook again. She pursed her lips in confusion, then left with the trays.

With a sigh of relief, Pak went out back to find Jack. At least Hardin was safe for the moment.

✳ ✳ ✳

"What next?" Jack said as Pak motioned for him to return down the alley to the car.

"We need to figure out what's in the food, but that can wait. Right now, we need to–"

"What's in the food?" Jack repeated, looking at the tray in his hand.

"Correct. The immediate crisis has been averted, at least until the cook wakes up and raises Cain, or the Koreans discover Hardin's food is having no effect on him."

"Hardin's food?" Jack said, turning pale.

"On the tray, yes," Pak said. He wheeled on Jack in sudden horror. "Jack! Did you...?"

"We didn't get breakfast, Pak. I thought you were bringing me breakfast."

Pak shuddered. "Jack, this is bad. Very bad. NOT the way to make your sponsor look good. Now we have to help Hardin... or you!"

"Maybe I'll be fine?" Jack said. "I mean, I only picked at it. Most of the stuff tastes really weird."

Pak shook his head. "We don't even know what it is. How toxic. If fatal or not. Wait! We need to make you throw up!"

"Throw up?" Jack said. "I have no idea how. I hate throwing up."

"Should have thought of that before eating poison, Jack. Stick your finger in your throat."

Jack put down the tray, leaned over, and stuck his finger in his mouth. He gagged and spit, but nothing came up. He shook his head. "Not working, Pak."

"If we had activated charcoal, you could be okay. Do you have activated charcoal?"

Jack shook his head. "No. Why would I have activated charcoal?"

"Perhaps because you often eat stupid things and require it?"

"No," Jack said, "No, I don't. You brought me a tray of food without explanation, then I tasted it."

"Throw up, Jack—don't argue! Just vomit!"

Jack tried again, with a weird gargling hiccup as he gagged unproductively.

"Throw up, Jack, throw up," he told himself.

"It's not working, Pak."

"Maybe I have to stick my finger in your throat?" Pak said.

"No, that's nasty. I'll keep trying." Jack tried again, but the spicy Korean breakfast refused to return. "It wasn't even that good to eat, Pak, and now I'm going to die. Great."

"This is because you are stupid, Jack. So, so stupid. I am angry with how stupid you are."

Jack flushed red but said nothing.

Then Pak had a sudden flash of insight. "Jack! Stick your head in stinking dumpster and think of vomit!"

"Pak?"

"Do it, Jack!"

Jack did, lifting the flap on the green receptacle. His eyes watered as he smelled the stench of millions of bacterial exudates. "Throw up, Jack, throw up," he told himself as he stared into a mess of rotten fish. "Throw up, throw up, throw up! Come on, vomit! Vomit, vomit, vomit, vomit!" Jack was yelling now, but he suddenly realized he shouldn't be yelling—the Koreans were right inside. Then Jack realized that Pak should have told him to stop yelling. He pulled his head out of the dumpster and looked behind him just in time to see a broad-shouldered Korean step over Pak's limp body and raise a polished club of *Fraxinus chinensis*.

CHAPTER SEVEN

All three of the Koreans were named Park. When Hardin asked if they were related, they all shook their heads yes, then no.

Hardin knew almost nothing about Koreans, their culture, or their food. These men had said very little to him, making him wonder if perhaps it was rude to speak before a meal. Not that it mattered. He was a direct to-the-point sort of a guy. An American businessman, born and bred, just like his father, owner of Hardin's Bicycles back in Cincinnati. He hadn't shared his father's interest in wheels, preferring to collect rocks and hunt for arrowheads. He had decided to join the Army and was later recruited for F.O.R.E.S.T. due to his interest in geology. That had been a dangerous decade. After meeting his wife, Hardin took an early retirement and started AgriTweak.

AgriTweak had grown from a little in-house operation run by Hardin and his wife to a solid, nationally known lab. It was still small, having only a half-dozen employees, but Hardin was definitely ready to make the international jump, fire or no fire. When the Koreans had shown up offering to help him move into the massive Asian market, he had jumped at the chance.

He wondered, however, why they weren't doing it themselves. Something seemed a bit "off" about these fellows and he was starting to wonder if this was going to be a waste of time. South Korea wasn't known for its lack of high-tech manufacturing capabilities. He remembered when Korean cars were scoffed at. Now they had a significant market share, even in the US. *Maybe soil sampling just isn't that interesting to a high-tech culture? Perhaps they're ashamed of their farming past and are attempting to jump directly into consumerist technocracy?*

"So, Mr. Park, you wanted to talk about what AgriTweak can do for you?" Hardin asked the Korean he thought was in charge.

The man nodded and said, "Yes, yes, Mr. Hardin. I am quite interested indeed." The three men nodded together.

The waitress brought out a tray of tea and a single cup of coffee for Hardin, along with packets of sugar and a little bowl of cream. "Thank you," Hardin said, adding a splash of cream to his coffee and taking a sip. It wasn't particularly good, but it raised a strange sense of nostalgia in him. It reminded him of rotisserie hot dog machines, fake nacho cheese, and parked 18-wheelers.

The Koreans sipped their tea and said nothing. The waitress sat on a stool at a little front desk, running through numbers on a ticker-tape calculator. *This is awkward*, Hardin thought. The minutes crept by. Eventually, the waitress slid down from her stool and wandered back to the kitchen again. A moment later, she emerged with trays of food.

She placed dishes carefully on the table in front of each man, serving Hardin last. The spread was pungent and completely unfamiliar to Hardin. It smelled like sauerkraut, and some of it looked like it could be sauerkraut. "Eat, Mr. Hardin. Enjoy. You try Korean food—very good for you. Very good!" Park I stated. Park II and Park the driver both nodded in unison with big smiles. "Enjoy!"

Hardin took a tentative bite of a crunchy yellow slice. On first taste, it was rather like a pickle—but then a blast of heat hit his mouth like a cross between mustard and habaneros. He took a swig of his coffee, but the heat made the sting worse—much worse. There was no water at the table. *Do Koreans not drink water?* He didn't want to appear weak in front of them, but he was pretty sure they could tell he was sweating and tearing up.

Rice, Hardin thought. *I'll eat some rice.* He took a few big bites of rice in succession after pushing aside the shredded seaweed-looking material on top of it, in case that also was laced with something unpleasant. He rolled the rice around inside his mouth, trying to scrub his tongue with it.

"Enjoying your meal, Mr. Hardin?" asked Park II.

Hardin nodded, his mouth too stuffed with rice to respond. He was pretty sure Park was making fun of him. *Well, if that's the way they want to roll, that's their problem. Is ritual humiliation of potential clients a standard part of Korean business dealings?* Hardin swallowed the rice. Most of the burn was gone, but a sip of coffee brought it back.

The waitress suddenly raced in from the kitchen again and said something sharp in Korean. "One moment," Park II said to Hardin. "Please still eat—very sorry. Will be right back." All three Parks vanished into the kitchen after the waitress.

Hardin looked at his plate. The only thing he knew for sure was safe was the rice, and that was almost gone. He was still hungry, though, so he took a tentative bite of the seaweed. It wasn't bad. Not really. Kind of nutty and salty. There was a little bit of pepper in it but nothing like the crunchy yellow things. He tried a bite of something he thought might be pork. It was sweet and good, so he carefully removed all crunchy yellow things from that portion of his plate and scooped the supposed pig meat into the section with the rice. *Now this is progress*, he thought, though he still wished for a normal American breakfast.

Bacon and eggs and a few flapjacks, maybe. And good coffee. And orange juice, and maybe a bit of oatmeal with butter and salt. That really was the best way to eat oatmeal.

He was polishing off the safe portions of his meal when the three Koreans returned.

"Very sorry, Mr. Hardin," said Park I.

"No problem, I hope?" said Hardin.

"No, no problem. Woman just needed a little help moving something in kitchen."

"I helped," all three of them said together.

"But no problem now." said Park III. "You are enjoying your food?"

"Yes," Hardin lied, "yes, very good. Thank you."

"Eat some more of the pickles?"

"No, thank you. No, I'm sure I'm quite full. Not really much of a breakfast guy," Hardin lied again. He knew he shouldn't lie, and usually prided himself on his honesty, but this meal really required some lying.

He noticed the three men were looking at him intently. He put down his fork and took a swig of coffee, then stared back at them.

"So, are you gentlemen ready to talk business? This has been nice, but I do wish to get back to the conference before missing too much of the day's events."

"Of course, sir," said Park I. "And you are feeling quite well? The food, it agrees with you?"

"Yes, fine."

The men really were looking at him strangely. This was all getting too bizarre and he was ready to fish or cut bait.

"What? What is it? Are we talking business or what?"

"Yes, Mr. Hardin. Tell me, what do you know about top men in agriculture industry?"

"Top men? What does that have to do with anything?"

"Well, Mr. Hardin, I see you are connected man. Important, yes, with a good set of clients. I also wish to know these clients and friends as we expand ourselves."

"I don't see what my client list has to do with the deal you said we were going to make, but I've worked with agricultural extensions, some good-sized farms, a couple of agribiz outfits in Iowa, Kansas, Wisconsin..."

"I want names," the three men said at the same time.

"Are you not feeling like you want to share with me more information, Mr. Hardin?" Park II said.

"No, I don't see why I would. This has really gotten to be ridiculous. I thought you guys wanted to talk business, not steal my Rolodex."

The Koreans looked at each other and nodded, then looked back at Hardin.

"Okay, this is fine," said Park I. "I will drive you back to hotel, okay?" Hardin was really irritated now. "I don't get it. You just wanted to buy me breakfast and talk about my client list? What about expanding internationally? How we can help you do whatever you're doing? What next—you want me to pay for your meals?"

Park III shook his head. "No, Mr. Hardin. Not for the meals. But you will pay, oh yes."

"I... what?"

✳ ✳ ✳

"Pak?" Jack said.

A muffled groan was the only reply.

"Pak," Jack said again, taking a quick kick at the figure tied up beside him. "It wasn't switchblades."

"Yeah, yeah, Jack, yeah," came the answer, groggily. "Wait... switchblades?"

"We're tied up, man—they got us. I thought they'd have switchblades, though."

"Got us?"

Pak woke up completely and realized he was tied up in the same utility room. The cook was no longer there. Pak tried to move but a wave of pain in his head almost blacked him out again. He felt for his trowel. It was gone.

"Jack," he said. "I think sponsoring you may have been a bad move on my part. Now we are both tied up and your boss will soon be dead."

"A bad move, Pak? Au contraire, my friend."

Pak looked up to see Jack standing above him, holding a meat cleaver. "Hold still—we're busting out."

A moment later, the two of them were loose.

"Foolish," said Pak. "They took my trowel but not the cleaver. These Koreans are odd."

He stood up, and a wave of pain flowed through him. It was all he could do to move. Carefully, he clutched the wall and looked into the kitchen. The cook was lying there on the floor, still out cold. That was strange—they must have moved him, then left him there to conclude the business with Hardin.

Pak realized there might still be time to reach him before the Koreans did whatever they were going to do.

"C'mon, Jack—let's get to the car."

As they pushed open the back door, Pak was amazed at their dumb luck. He woozily staggered down the alley. Jack seemed to be in better shape, but there was a nasty bruise on his forehead right between the eyes. Pak had to admit the cocky American was a tough character, even if he was wet behind the ears.

Except he had thrown the leg of a love seat through a man's chest. Right through. Underestimating the man was obviously foolish.

They moved down the alley like two drunks, much worse for the wear, reaching the car.

Though Pak hated to say it, he was really in no condition to drive.

"Jack, can you drive?"

Jack nodded. "I'm feeling a little strange but I think my balance and everything is better than yours, Pak."

"Strange, Jack?"

"Yeah, like, well," Jack squinted. "Yeah, you have a halo right now."

"A halo?"

"Like an angel, Pak. You look like an angel. Like one of those ceramic ones you'd see in the Christian bookstore, in between the myrrh essential oils and the real authentic shofars. Just to the left of the *Three Little Pigs Meet The Thankful Leper* board book."

Pak shook his head. "Jack, I really don't think you should drive, you really sound..." he said, trailing off as the shaking of his head brought a rush of pain and he slumped against the side of the car.

"Get in, bud," Jack said, propping him up and shoving him into the vehicle. "We're gonna save my boss."

* * *

"So I am very sorry, Mr. Hardin," Park II said. "I do want to talk some business but have been very distracted. I can talk now."

They were back in the car, driving into town. Hardin just nodded at Park II. He was done with this nonsense.

"I just have to stop for a moment and get other car. One moment," said Park I as they pulled into a warehouse building with unreadable oriental characters on the side.

The three Parks stepped out of the smart car and motioned for Hardin to do the same.

Park the driver unlocked a warehouse bay. Inside was a large off-road truck.

Park I and II spoke at the same time "I must go now, Hardin. Big business calls. I are sorry I could not talk more with you, but you are not very important to big plans. Goodbye."

Hardin gave a half-wave. Park III started the truck and asked Hardin to get in.

Hardin did, and they were off.

A few moments later, he realized they were no longer heading into town. The road stretched off ahead of them into the desert. He looked at the driver, now very suspicious.

"Hey, listen—where are we going?"

"I am returning you."

"Returning me? To the hotel? This is the wrong way!"

"The hotel? No, no. Returning you to..."

...the driver pulled an AMS EZ Eject Soil Probe from beside his seat and pointed it at Hardin...

"...our mother, the earth!"

Then he stabbed it into Hardin's chest.

✳ ✳ ✳

"They went in there!" Pak said as Jack tailed the smart car. It had turned into a fenced warehouse area. "Just pull past in a casual way."

"Past the zoo?" Jack said.

"Past what?" said Pak. "What zoo?"

"Those hippos look mad, Pak. Really mad."

Pak looked at Jack. This wasn't good.

"Some of them are getting inside my head," Jack said.

Jack had now pulled past the lot and parked a block up the road in front of a run-down mechanic shop of some sort. In front of it stood a tire sculpture in the shape of a man. At some point in the past it probably looked whimsical. Now it looked pathetic, as the peeling paint and missing arm on one side spoke of a business no longer in good health, if still extant at all.

As they had rolled past the Korean warehouse, however, Pak had peered through the car window and saw Hardin getting into a truck as two of the other men got back into the smart car.

"Pak?" said Jack.

Pak looked at Jack just as he explosively vomited Korean food all across the dash and front seats, barely missing Pak himself.

"I need to throw up."

CHAPTER EIGHT

Pak was driving now, with the windows down. The truck carrying Hardin had headed off the road and across the desert.

Jack was scratching his arms and muttering about bull ants. When Jack had spotted the tire man, he'd become convinced it was a "skunk ape". "Musk glands!" he shouted at Pak, "Musk glands!"

Pak had traded seats with Jack just before the truck passed. He hunched low, in case the driver spotted them. He apparently hadn't, as the truck kept driving. In the rear view, he saw the Smart car receding in the opposite direction. He started the Fiesta and headed after the truck, keeping a long tailing distance.

It was obvious that the Fiesta was not designed for off-roading, though it held the ground admirably well for a two-wheel drive. The banging inside was almost intolerable, however, Jack seemed to have settled down a bit. Now he was pretending to share cake with a strangely invisible person.

"So skinny," he said. "Can barely see you, girl..."

Pak heard a nasty bang, then suddenly the car's engine sounded a lot louder. He had been staying far behind the truck but they must have spotted him by now. There was nothing else to see and a white car isn't exactly easy to hide in the desert. He lost sight of the truck repeatedly, then would see it again as he went over a ridge.

The loud sound must be the muffler, Pak thought. *Or the lack thereof.*

He used to live in a neighborhood where a local teen had a little Honda with a round back on it. *What was that type of Honda called,* Pak thought. *A fastback?* Anyhow, the kid had taken off the muffler and run it. Very, very loud. He then put some other kind of muffler on it. A lemon bomb. No, "lemon balm" was an herb. Cherry bomb. It was a cherry bomb! That made the car's little 4-cylinder engine sound like a massive V8... sort of. It was loud. *Yes, we definitely must have lost the muffler.*

His thoughts were interrupted by another explosion, followed by a repeated banging. The car skidded sideways. *Rental agency will not be happy*, thought Pak, *though at least I have not added tractor-related decals to the windows.*

"My date exploded," yelled Jack, then burst into tears. "Oh, so young... so thin..."

Now we're not going to catch the truck, Pak thought, getting out of the car and looked at the destroyed back tire. Jack fumbled with his door and staggered out as well, leaning heavily on the side of the Fiesta.

"What now?" he panted. He really looked ill.

"Jack, we are rescuing Hardin. We need to get out and see if we can see where truck goes. Stay here—I'll be back."

Pak set off up a small ridge and then looked down to see what he could see.

From the top he spied the dust rising where the truck has passed, and far off—there it was. It was... stopping?

Sure enough, the truck came to a halt. A barely distinguishable figure stepped out of the driver's side, then walked around to the passenger door and opened it. In horror, Pak watched as the figure pulled out a limp form.

Hardin was already dead!

Pak turned around and looked down to see Jack had collapsed on the ground next to the Fiesta. He raced down the hill to his friend, face-down in the dust.

He rolled Jack onto his back. His eyes were open, staring into the sky, pupils wide open. *That can't be good for his eyes*, Pak thought, shading Jack's face with his hand. He felt like passing out himself but to do that now might kill them both. He noticed Jack was sweating heavily in the heat. *Perhaps he was also dehydrated, along with the action of the drug?* He slapped Jack's face lightly, spoke to him, rubbed his hands—nothing. No response.

He carefully turned Jack's head to the side so he wasn't staring up into the blazing sun, then went back to the car to see if there was any water. Nothing. He wondered if he could get water out of the radiator, then decided it was almost certainly too hot at the moment.

Then he heard it. *The truck!*

Pak raced back up the ridge again and looked down—it was heading right towards them. If he saw Jack, he would almost certainly run him over.

Pak looked around. There had to be something he could do to stop the truck. It was perhaps a quarter mile away. He was sure the Korean was coming back to finish them all off. That had to be it. He must have seen the Fiesta. Pak was sure that was the case. It wasn't like little white cars drove out into the desert off-road every day. At least, he assumed they didn't.

"JACK!" Pak yelled from the top of the ridge, just in case his friend could be awakened. "GET OUT OF THE WAY!"

No luck. Looking around, Pak noted the fallen remains of a tree. He wondered if he could break a piece of it off and roll it down the hill in front of the truck and maybe somehow derail its forward progress. Hard to say. Probably not. He only had a few seconds.

Then he wondered: could he fell a saguaro in the truck's path? There was nothing to cut it with, though. Yet perhaps if he built up enough inertia? *No time to think!* He ran towards a cactus, slamming both feet into it with a side kick. It fell, pulling out a small clump of roots. Pak shoved against its side, dodging the spines and straining and pushing until the massive cactus was moving.

The chances of it hitting the incoming truck were a thousand to one—he was sure he couldn't make it happen but had to try.

The truck was seconds away! With a final heave, the saguaro started rolling down the hillside. It was going to miss! It was going...

...right in front of the truck! As it rushed past, the driver swung his speeding truck to one side, slamming into an outcropping of stone in a hail of gravel and dust. The truck barely stayed upright as the radiator exploded in a hiss of steam.

Yeah, definitely a good idea that I didn't open the radiator on the car, Pak thought.

But the driver was unharmed! The driver leapt from the car holding some sort of a strange weapon. Pak hissed involuntarily—it was a soil sampler! But for the quick-eject lever on the side, it looked like the incredibly lethal 33" AMS EZ Kleen 1-1/8" diameter with the heat-treated tip. The addition of the quick eject feature made the tool perfect for repeated samplings—or kills! The Korean walked over to Jack's prone form and looked about. He moved Jack's head with his boot so he could look into his face.

"You!" the Korean said, obviously recognizing Jack—though Pak had no idea how. He set off down the hill as fast as he dared, hoping he'd reach his friend in time.

CHAPTER NINE

Jack sat in the food court of a pleasant indoor mall. Light streamed in from skylights overhead. *A little too bright*, he thought, but the air conditioning was keeping up. He couldn't remember how he got here but he was glad to be out of the desert.

He was looking at a menu boasting "37 Flavors of Ice Cream". The flavors didn't look promising so far. Pickled radish. Pickled radish with ginger. Pickled turmeric. Seaweed turmeric. Rice noodle. Pickled rice noodle with turmeric and radish.

His stomach lurched. He had eaten something before coming here. Something that didn't agree with him. One side of his face felt hot, too, despite the air conditioning.

Mustard pickle. Seaweed mustard. Red bean pickle. Red bean radish seaweed rice turmeric mustard pickle.

His stomach turned over with a bubbling sound and he put the menu down. Looking up, he realized he wasn't alone at his table.

HI, yelled the man across from him.

"Hi," said Jack. The man didn't look like he belonged in a food court. He was large and wizened, with big hands and thick fingernails and a long brown beard streaming down his ancient face. His eyes were deep green and he wore a coarsely spun robe.

I THOUGHT THIS WOULD BE A GOOD TIME TO TALK, said the man, in a harsh voice which was entirely too loud and masculine. He had a slight accent. *German, maybe?* The voice sounded familiar.

"Are you a wrestler?" asked Jack. "Let me guess. Your stage name is something like The Brown Wizard. Didn't I see you fight Mankind?"

The man shook his head.

NO. NOT A WRESTLER!

"Why are you so loud?" Jack said, wincing.

I DIDN'T REALIZE I WAS TOO LOUD. I LEARNED TO SPEAK AMERICAN FROM YOUR VIDEOS.

"English, you mean. And my what?" Jack said.

YOUR AWESOME FIGHT VIDEOS. VERY MUCH LIKED THEM. INTENSE!

Jack realized at this point he must be dreaming, so he pinched himself. Nothing happened. He pinched himself again but nothing changed.

Then the man across from him spoke again. Yelled, actually.

YOU'RE OUT COLD!

"Ah," said Jack. "I was starting to think this particular moment in time was stranger than most other moments I've experienced. You said you learned English from my fight videos? Not from listening to me?"

NO. EAVESDROPPING IS RUDE.

"Great. I think I'll just stop talking and wait until I wake up, if that's okay."

I NEED TO TELL YOU SOMETHING FIRST, said the wrestling wizard man.

"I hope you'll tell me where we can get better ice cream flavors."

SILENCE. TIME IS SHORT.

"Okay," said Jack, cocking an eyebrow. "I'll let you talk."

YOU MUST WONDER WHY I AM HERE WITH YOU.

"No," said Jack. "I figured that out already. It's because this is a dream."

NO, THAT IS NOT WHY. YOU WERE POISONED.

"Poisoned?" Jack's stomach lurched again. He began to remember a tray of strange food.

KOREANS POISONED YOU.

It came back to him. The food, then trying to throw up, a skunk ape, then disconnected images... and nothing.

"That's right—I remember now!"

AND YOU PASSED THROUGH INTO MY REALM. MORE THAN USUAL, THAT IS.

"Your realm? Are you—oh, shoot—are you a demon?"

NOT REALLY, said the old man.

"Good. I remember hearing that drugs can connect a person with the spirit world. Lots of nasty creatures over there, I've heard. Actually, I didn't hear it. I read it in a tract at my old church. A comic book tract. And really, I'm not really keen on being possessed or anything. Though technically you probably can't do that, me being a Christian. I was at church this last Sunday, and–"

SYCAMORES, said the man.

Jack blinked. That was right. *Maybe this was a demon. He had found a weak spot in Jack's faith and was exploiting it.*

"You were eavesdropping. You are a demon! Get behind me!" he yelled, holding up the menu like a crucifix.

NOW, NOW—NONE OF THAT. I AM NOT ATTACKING YOUR FAITH. I JUST REMEMBERED ABOUT THE SYCAMORE BECAUSE THAT BOTHERED ME TOO. IT IS NOT A BIG DEAL, THOUGH. REMEMBER, MOST PEOPLE DON'T CARE ABOUT THOSE DETAILS. THE WORLD OF PLANTS IS LESS IMPOR-TANT TO THEM. THAT IS WHY I AM SPEAKING TO YOU INSTEAD OF SOMEONE LIKE YOUR PASTOR.

"Because my pastor would cast you out?"

NO. STOP WITH THE DEMON STUFF. THAT IS NOT ME. I AM A GARDENER, LIKE YOURSELF. THOUGH MUCH OLDER.

"A gardener?"

The man held up his hands. *SEE THE DIRT UNDER MY NAILS?*

"Sure," said Jack, "but I also see a horrible list of ice cream flavors here. I don't believe in them, so why should I believe in your nails?"

WHO GAVE YOU THE POWER OVER PLANTS, JACK?

"Power?"

YES. YOU BROUGHT ME TO YOU. AH, FAIR KIIKALA! SO FEW REMEMBER.

Kiikala. *That was familiar. Wait—the turnip seed he had gotten from Niklas!*

"Turnips," Jack said. "You showed up because of my turnips?"

The wizard bowed slightly.

"And then gave me some powers?"

The wizard looked silently at Jack, his eyes like deep pools.

YES. YOU ARE THE CARETAKER, AND THUS I CARE FOR YOU. YOU REMEMBER THE WOOD?

"Wood? What in the world? What are you talking about?"

YOU THREW THE WOOD, AND I– WAIT–

"Wait? What?"

YOU NEED TO WAKE UP. NOW. AND ROLL OVER WHEN YOU DO. FAST!

"I need to wait, what?"

The man reached across the table and slapped Jack's face.

CHAPTER TEN

Jack snapped awake, rolling over as he had been told. Metal glinted above him and drove down through the edge of his shirt, scratching his side as it dug into the ground. If he hadn't rolled, it would have pierced his chest. Struggling, he looked up at a dark and blurry silhouette as it yanked back the implement. *No—it couldn't be—was it?* Jack's attacker looked just like his mom.

Then Pak arrived and swung into action.

Park III screamed in pain as an expertly slung and exquisitely spiny pad of *Opuntia* hit him full in the face. Pak followed with the flying kick and double punch known as the "thrice-flooded paddy," knocking the Korean headlong into a boulder. The would-be Jack assassin now lay limp on the rocky ground.

"Pak, why did you do that!" yelled Jack, getting up from the ground.

"Jack—I saved your life!"

"Saved my life? By hitting my MOM? I don't think so!"

Jack took a wild swing at Pak, who dodged with ease. Years of hand-to-hand combat without pulled punches had honed his skills. Jack's fury came to an abrupt end as Pak swept his friend's legs out from underneath him and put him in a hold.

"You just... you just... can't hit my mom, Pak!"

"Stop, Jack, stop. You are insane right now. We will get you home. Later you will see your mom, and she is not this man here. This Korean doesn't even look like you. Or like a woman. It is very obvious when you are not on drugs."

"Pak!"

"I'll take care of him, Jack."

"MY MOM IS NOT A MAN!"

"You just stay here. If I let go, will you stay here?"

Jack half-nodded, his face in the dirt, and Pak let go.

Jack rose and looked at the fallen form of the person who had tried to stab him. He slowly realized it wasn't his mom. He wondered about the other man he'd been talking to in the food court. The Brown Wizard. Was he real? *Probably not*, Jack thought, confusedly. The sky and the hills were spinning. He looked down at the ground until the spinning stopped.

✳ ✳ ✳

"I'm sorry, Pak," Jack said slowly. "I was in the food court and woke suddenly. All the ice cream flavors were awful."

Pak nodded in understanding as he bent over the fallen Korean. "Sometimes one must stick with the classics. Or Neapolitan, which combines all three."

Park's pulse was strong, though he had a strange, earthy aroma about him. Pak had no time to wonder. They had to get out of here. *Jack should drink something*, he thought as he walked back to the truck. The steam had stopped, but the engine was still running, now making a dangerous knocking sound. He opened the door and turned it off. Inside, he found a thermos of tea—hot, but it would have to do. He handed Jack the thermos. Jack opened it and took a sip, then a gulp.

They were in trouble. One vehicle had a popped tire and the other had a broken radiator. And they were in the middle of nowhere. He wondered how far the truck would go before overheating. Probably only a mile or two. And if he kept pushing, the engine block would eventually overheat and crack. Then they might all die in the wilderness. Not good.

Then again...

Pak pulled his phone out of his pocket. Two bars. *That's why I pay for the good service*, he thought. He turned on location services and pulled up their coordinates on Google maps.

Jack was now lying on his side, panting. He still looked pretty ill. Pak wished he had some activated charcoal. At least Jack wasn't raving at the moment.

The sun beat down relentlessly from above. It was one thing to drive through the desert with the AC cranked—it was another to run up and down ridges, attempting to roll cactuses in front of speeding trucks, then engage their drivers in hand-to-hand combat. As if summoned, the Korean moaned softly.

Pak couldn't just call the police in on this one. He needed information from the Korean—and he still had to go see what had happened with Hardin. If only Jack hadn't eaten breakfast!

With a deep sigh, Pak pressed a button on his speed dial which he really, really didn't want to press. The phone rang and a faraway voice answered.

✳ ✳ ✳

As he neared the location where he had seen Hardin dumped from the car, Pak could not see the body, though there was some blood on the ground. The area was rocky, with plenty of cracks and crevasses.

Hmm... I wonder if... an animal could have?

Then something whipped across Pak's back, scratching him painfully as it tore his shirt. He spun around and found Hardin, clutching his chest with one hand while brandishing a *Senegalia greggii* branch in the other. Pak jumped back as Hardin prepared to bring the branch down on him a second time. "Stop it, you fool!" he yelled. "I've had enough of Koreans for one day, punk!" Hardin rasped back at him.

"No—I am Chinese!"

"Then I've had enough of Asians!"

"Russians are Asians too," Pak gasped, holding his bleeding head with one hand and raising the other to ward off the blow he felt must be incoming. "So are Israelis. And Maldivians. People often miss that fact."

"Oriental Asians, I mean. I mean..."

Pak looked at him.

"I mean, I'm sorry, I know you aren't supposed to say "oriental" anymore, but hey, look, you guys tried to kill me."

"Not me!" said Pak, through gritted teeth. "I'm here to save you."

"Save me?" Hardin lowered the branch a fraction of an inch.

"You are in grave danger. Or, were in grave danger. Look at you—you are injured and have no real options other than to trust me. Are you going to hit me with that stick or not?"

Hardin shrugged and threw it away. "I guess not."

Pak smiled wryly. "I should have expected a former agent of F.O.R.E.S.T. would be tough."

"How do you know about that?" Hardin asked. His eyes narrowed.

Pak shrugged. "We have similar interests. However, I am glad to see you alive. I thought you'd be dead."

Hardin cocked an eyebrow at him. "Dead?"

"Yes. Like the others."

"Others?" Hardin echoed.

"Long story, boss man. We need to get back to the others." He offered his arm to Hardin.

Hardin nodded, slumping against him. "I am sorry. Really thought you were Korean."

"Koreans look completely different, Hardin."

"I..."

"No time to talk. We need to get you out of this heat and stop the bleeding. We also need to go back to Jack before he decides to fight a cactus or something."

"Jack?"

∗ ∗ ∗

When they got back to the little valley, Hardin was amazed to see it was in fact his Jack, breaker of vending machines and soil grinders. Jack was on the ground, staring at Hardin as if he were a ghost.

"Pak—am I hallucinating again?"

"Jack, how are you here? How are you mixed up in this business?" Hardin sputtered. "Are you okay, are you–" He coughed, painfully, unable to complete the sentence.

"It's no use talking with him, Hardin," Pak volunteered. "He's on drugs."

"Drugs?" Hardin wheezed, "I would have expected better from you, Jack."

"I threw up in the car," Jack slurred.

Hardin shook his head slowly. "Your father... would be sad to hear it... drugs? You've got a whole life ahead of you, but... you turned to drugs?"

"He did not turn to drugs," Pak said. "He was drugged."

"He was drugged?" Hardin gasped. "What do you mean?"

"By Koreans, Mr. Hardin. The drugs were intended for you."

Hardin's mouth fell open. "Wait, me, what?"

"Sit down, Mr. Hardin. You shouldn't be speaking. Relax," Pak said, helping Hardin sit in the limited shade beside the Korean's smashed truck. "We tailed you to the restaurant. We knew you were in trouble." Seeing Hardin's questioning look, Pak continued, "No time to explain how we knew. But Jack got the meal intended for you."

"I never... saw Jack... in the restaurant," Hardin said weakly. "How did he... get my meal?"

Pak's phone rang.

"Can't say now, must answer phone. You need to rest."

"Who is it?" Jack said.

Pak held up a finger as he spoke into the receiver with a string of Mandarin.

He then hung up and said something that sounded suspiciously like a curse.

"Never mind who. We will have a ride soon."

There was no way—no way at all—that Pak was going to admit he had called his mother for help.

✳ ✳ ✳

Jack sat cross-legged beside Hardin against the truck. Hardin breathed with difficulty, blood seeping through his shirt. Pak had left about fifteen minutes before, telling them to keep an eye on each other. Jack kept seeing elves out of the corner of his eyes, but every time he turned his head they were gone. He wished they would make him some cookies.

There was a soft crunch of footsteps approaching. It was Pak, carrying a fistful of feathery leaves.

"Oh that poor elf!" Jack whimpered as Pak unbuttoned Hardin's shirt and pressed a small, dead figure in green against Hardin's wound.

"Jack, shush. This is a plant, not a fairy-tale creature. You remember what this is, right?"

Pak held up a feathery leaf so Jack could see it. Jack's eyes cleared and he nodded.

"*Achillea millefolium!* Stops bleeding."

"Very good," Pak said. "You're not all the way out of it. Though I would venture to call this *Achillea lanulosa*."

Jack shook his head. "It's highly variable. *A. lanulosa* is likely just a regional variation of *A. millefolium*, not a species in its own right."

Pak shrugged. "Whatever you prefer."

"What are you guys... talking about?" Hardin muttered. "I'm so cold."

"He's going into shock," Pak said to Jack. "We don't have much time."

The sound of an engine bubbled up into Pak's consciousness. A vehicle was nearby.

"Here—keep this pressed onto the wound, Jack," Pak said, handing the wad of yarrow leaves to his friend. "If you see anything weird, ignore it."

He climbed up the ridge and saw a trail of dust approaching, kicked up by the wheels of what appeared to be a station wagon. Pak took a stick from the ground and waved it in the air to flag down the driver. It worked, as the vehicle changed course for their direction.

The vehicle appeared to be a Subaru. Four-wheel drive, Pak assumed. It wasn't driving particularly fast—which was good. He hoped it would be spared the same fate as the Fiesta. Finally, the car pulled up in their midst, a soft cloud of dust drifting across them as the driver put the vehicle into park, cut the engine, opened the door and stepped out.

It was a Chinese woman in black, her hair dyed a brilliant red-purple color.

"Pak," she barked, seeing him. "Your mom NOT happy!"

Pak shook his head, yet again unleashing a wave of pain.

"Your mom?" said Jack. "Is this your mom?"

The woman wheeled on Jack. "I younger than him! You can't tell? You blind?"

Jack shrugged.

"No, Pak call his mom. She call me come pick him up. He's in trooouble!" she sang.

Pak winced, but ignored her as he and Jack lifted Hardin into the car. Jack took shotgun with a wink at the girl.

Then Pak walked away.

"Pak—where are you going?" said Jack after him.

"I'm going to get our Korean friend."

"Are you sure you don't want to leave him in the desert to be picked clean by vultures?"

"No," said Pak over his shoulder. "I have plans for him." He returned a moment later, hauling the unconscious man.

"Pop the trunk," he said to the woman.

"You stuff that man in my trunk!?" she said.

"It's okay, he's Korean. Now if you would please open it."

She did, and he unceremoniously dumped the man in. He slammed closed the trunk, walked around to the back and sat next to Hardin.

"Okay, Li, let's go."

"Ha," she said. "You should say please! You don't even say please? Even after I drive all this way and let you stuff man in trunk?"

"Just drive, Li. Get us back to town."

Li sniffed but started the car, turned, and started back towards civilization.

Jack was staring at her.

"What are you looking at?" she said.

"You're almost as skinny as my last girlfriend."

Li eyed him narrowly. "What happened to her?"

"She exploded."

"Well, maybe you told her she look like someone mom. That make girl explode."

"Maybe. I can't really remember very clearly," Jack admitted. "I ate some Korean food, and..."

"Korean food! Ha!" she interrupted. "No wonder you act crazy— you ARE crazy!"

* * *

"They're going to think you're dead, which is good," Pak said to Hardin, who sat limply beside him, staring out the window and breathing shallowly. The bleeding had mostly stopped, but he was pale and trembling. "But you need to stay alive," Pak continued. "Hang on."

It was hard to hear, as Li had cranked up the stereo. The music—if it was music—sounded like someone sliding an ancient glass door back and forth over a corroded rail. The volume dipped as the announcer's voice boomed in.

"You're listening to WNSE—THE NOISE! Coming up next, an-other solid block of static, followed by Cage in the Afternoon, then we celebrate the daily drive home with The 8-Bit After Work! Stream the noise online 24/7 at WNSEthenoise.com/bringthenoise..."

"I love this channel," Li said, "but this car not have right speaker system for best sound reproduction."

Jack nodded. "I suppose noise-canceling headphones would be a bad bet?"

She stuck out her tongue at him.

"Stay awake," Pak said to Hardin loudly. "I think you will live, but they must keep thinking you are dead, at least until we get to the bottom of all this."

Hardin nodded.

Pak continued. "I am not privy to the inner circles of the men who attacked you, but I imagine they are making a list and checking it twice, as you might say."

"So what... does this mean... for me, Pak?" he whispered. "Or my wife? Is she... a target? Could she... even now?"

"Unlikely," Pak replied, "as the pattern has been to leave the families out of this. So far. It is not beneath them, I think, but so far has not been the case."

Jack grinned at Li. "You are pretty, like a gazelle," he yelled over the noise. She snorted at him. Jack felt drunk. Something in his head told him to shut up, but he couldn't. "And you drive fast. I like fast women."

She stuck her tongue out at him again, but Jack could tell she liked him.

Hardin spoke to Pak again. "Listen, friend—you're saying... I need to lay low? What if... I get better... by tomorrow? There's a course... I'd really like... to play through. Maybe... just 9 holes, though."

Pak pursed his lips and started to shake his head, then realized for the hundredth time that head movements were not conducive to proper functioning. For a second he felt the urge to vomit. Head injuries were not good. He worried about IQ loss, then figured he actually had points to spare a few and still function quite decently. *Maybe I could get a regular job with less risk of head injury. Or where IQ doesn't matter. Politics, perhaps.* What was Hardin saying? Something about golf?

"Golf? In public? No, not now. Wrong people will think you are dead, then you will not be dead. Then they will make you dead. And you're not going to be in any shape to play golf soon. But keeping thinking positively."

Hardin frowned. "What about... the awards ceremony?"

Pak smiled. This guy was tough. "I think you should just lay low. Relax."

Hardin shrugged, then winced in pain. "Well, if you think I shouldn't go... well, I guess I shouldn't. Though... I don't know... who you are... or why I should trust you." With a jerk of his thumb he indicated Jack in the front seat. "But... judging by the company you keep... you're probably okay."

Pak nodded, and another wave of pain went through him. "He is a good guy, boss. Good guy. Can grow some very nice gardens, even if over-fond of soil disruption."

Hardin grimaced as he spoke "Soil disruption... really is necessary... for best results... in annual crops."

Pak nearly shook his head, but caught himself—the quickest yet!

"No, there is another way. No-till. But you should save your energy, Mr. Hardin."

Hardin waved a hand weakly. "No, no-till... certainly grown in popularity... but not nearly as efficient," he said, quietly and with obvious pain in his voice. "'There's another step of herbicide application, plus you need to adjust equipment for planting into crop wastes. Also, many root crops need that deep loosening... wouldn't you say?"

Pak remembered not to nod or shake his head this time. He wondered if perhaps he could train himself not to make head movements, then get better, then never make head movements again. Like some sort of robot.

"You only scratch the surface of your knowledge, Mr. Hardin. Only the surface. Literally. That guy in the back, bouncing around very uncomfortably in the trunk, I hope." Pak grinned. "He would say that disruption is genocide."

"Genocide?"

Pak almost nodded again. "I really cannot say more, really, must not say anything. I wish for you to forget this entire thing."

"Forget? I don't think I will forget that terrible..." He gasped, lips pale. "Breakfast. Followed by a forced ride... into the desert, then being stabbed with a...! That guy stabbed me with a soil probe, didn't he?"

"Yes," Pak said, "he would consider that poetic justice. Listen, Mr. Hardin—if you do much prying, they will try again. And Jack and I will not be around to save you. I beg of you, for your own safety, do not involve the authorities. This goes much higher than the police can manage."

"Yes...?"

"Yes. If you involve the police, they may disappear as well. These people will kill without hesitation on behalf of their beliefs."

"Who are you then?" Hardin said, almost whispering. "FBI? CIA?" Pak shook his head sharply, and a wave of nausea swept over him. He rolled down the window and threw up down the side of the bouncing Subaru, unleashing another wave of pain in his throbbing head.

This day really should be memorialized as a National Vomiting Day, or something.

∗ ∗ ∗

"Jack," Hardin whispered. Over the noise on the stereo, Jack couldn't hear him, but Pak did.

"Li! Turn off the noise," he said, tapping her on the shoulder. She complained, but Pak shushed her. "Hardin wants to speak to you, Jack," Pak said. "We're losing him."

The world was swimming around Jack. Between the desert outside, the crazy radio station, and the bumpy car ride, something had kicked off even more aftereffects of whatever poison he ingested. Jack tried to focus, knowing that Hardin needed him.

"Jack," Hardin said, reaching forward weakly. Jack took his hand. His formerly tough boss was trembling and sweaty.

"Jack, I think I was too hard on you."

Jack nodded.

"It was only that, well, you remind me of myself," Hardin continued, "before I became serious about life. You see, I also was a bit of a screwup. I didn't care for other people's equipment, you know, I just..."

Jack began to dislike this conversation.

"Well, I was a ne'er-do-well. Raised in a good family, but irresponsible. Bad at managing time, more interested in my own projects. Grating to others..."

Jack was now distinctly annoyed with this conversation.

"Really, a lot like you. I was not reliable. I had bad breath, smelled like junk food, was lousy with women, had a touch of scoliosis..."

"Enough," Jack said. "I get the idea."

Hardin closed his eyes. "But I believe in you, Jack. You have great potential. I know you can be something, something amazing." His voice was fading, but he gripped Jack's hand tightly. "Make me a promise."

"Sure," Jack said, "anything!"

"Avenge me."

Jack frowned. "No offense, but people don't normally dedicate their lives to avenging their bosses, even when their bosses are long-time personal friends."

"But Jack..." said Hardin. "Surely you can... fit it in... somewhere."

"Look, maybe I just need some time to think it through, Mr. Hardin?"

"Think it...?"

"Think it through. It's a big deal. If I decide to spend my life seeking vengeance, how much time am I really going to get in the garden?"

Pak glared. "Jack, he most likely is dying. You should just agree."

"Come on, Pak," Jack said. "You don't just do everything you're told because it's someone's dying wish." He looked to Li for support. Li looked back with accusation in her eyes.

"Wow," Jack said. "Everyone is against me on this? I just hoped to move to a jungle and marry a village full of wives and collect exotic plants, but all of you think I need to dedicate myself to killing insane Korean cultists?"

"He has dying wish, Jack!" said Li.

"Fine!" Jack said, squeezing Hardin's hand. "Fine, okay! Mr. Hardin, I vow to avenge you. If that's really what you want, then fine. I pledge my life to killing insane Korean cultists."

Even as he said the words, Jack felt his boss's hand go limp, and he wondered if Hardin had heard him. *Did it count if he didn't hear it?*

＊ ＊ ＊

Hardin had heard Jack, but as his spirit departed, ascended, looking down on the car and the desert receding below, revenge seemed unimportant. The barrens looked so much like the dusty Martian lands from his daydreams, so long ago.

CHAPTER ELEVEN

"He's gone, Jack." Pak removed his fingers from Hardin's throat. "We could not save him."

Jack was numb. He still felt very strange from whatever had poisoned him. He could hardly remember where he was or what he was doing, but he knew that letting Hardin die meant that he had failed his mission, and that he'd lost his last connection to his father.

"I blew it," he said to Pak.

"No, Jack. We did our best. Instead of dying alone, your friend died among people doing their best to care for him. And you swore to avenge him. Always a good way to move on."

"I hate to break manly conversation up, but we near town," Li said. "You might start think what you do with body of Hardin."

"Right, Li—we cannot simply bring the body to the police. We must... interview the Korean in the trunk, without delay, before anyone else dies needlessly."

"We have to bury Hardin," Jack said.

"Put some place safe. Then call police anonymous," said Li.

Pak agreed. "We will leave him in the park."

"The park?" Jack asked. In return, Pak pointed to a road sign reading "Ely Badger State Park."

Jack nodded, then closed his eyes, hoping the floor would stop melting beneath his feet.

✳ ✳ ✳

They left the body on the bench in a chained-off baseball dugout. Jack dragged it up the sidewalk along the baseball diamond with Li's help—Pak was too sick to assist. Leaving Mr. Hardin on the bench felt wrong to Jack, but he did not know what else could be done. More people were going to die—and soon—if they couldn't track down the killers.

Jack looked down at the body of the man who had been his surrogate father. He was more peaceful in death. His endless energy and drive had gone—had been stolen—leaving only the shell. Jack laid his hand on Hardin's head, and he prayed for success in his vengeance, and he walked away.

Li took them back to their hotel. Taking the Korean inside turned out to be a bit of a trick.

"You hold one side, Jack," Pak said, "and you, Li, get the other."

"I've got him," said Jack. The effects of the drug were receding, and he was seeing only slight halos around people, lights and, strangely, objects starting with the letter "A".

They decided on the direct approach, so they simply walked through the lobby, dragging their limp burden. Many businessmen were wandering about, most obviously in the agricultural industry. The ratio of John Deere paraphernalia to population was significantly higher than in the outside world.

"That boy have a little too much to drink?" one large-bellied man in an ill-fitting suit and cowboy hat asked.

Li nodded. "Can't handle his Coors Light," she quipped.

She and Jack hauled the Korean into the elevator as Pak held the door. Some of the businessmen laughed. One pointed at Pak, "Looks like you got in a fight there, bud."

Pak nodded and almost fell over. "Yes, yes, bad fight. My friend always talks, how you say? Smack. Yes. He always talk smack when he drink, then pass out and leave me get beat up. Very unfortunate. Silver bullet actually slow you down."

The businessman looked puzzled.

"And it fill you up," Pak continued. "With injuries."

They dropped the Korean in Pak and Jack's room, then Li left, promising to alert the police where to find Hardin's body. They locked the door behind her.

"Let us hope I did not kill him," Pak said to Jack. "Head injuries are tricky. Not all big hammers coming down on heads, bumps rising, then coyote running 100 miles per hour and all fine again in next scene."

"What?" said Jack, looking at the glowing alarm clock beside the bed.

"Never mind. Please, go get me some ice from the machine, Jack. My own head is not in good shape."

Jack looked at Pak. He skin was green underneath his halo.

"Yeah, you look terrible, bud. My head also hurts, so ice isn't a bad idea."

Jack studied himself in the mirror. He also looked terrible. His left eye was bloodshot. There was an angry blue-black mark on his forehead, and his face was stubbly. The Band-Aid had peeled half off of his cheek, revealing an ugly red scratch and a gummy black outline from the adhesive. He splashed his face with water, wincing at the pain in his head. Then he grabbed the little ice bucket, which was a nauseating shade of pink, left the room, and headed down to the common area.

Someone was already there, getting ice. It was the woman, from the hallway, from before. She was wearing a light little breezy dress. She had the earbuds in again.

Jack stood behind her in the doorway, watching her fill an ice bucket. When she finished, she turned and started to walk past him, but then looked back and pulled out her earbuds. "You're the guy with the... the... SPCA?"

Jack grinned.

"What happened to your face?" she continued. "It's worse."

"What happened to *your* face?" Jack retorted.

She narrowed her eyes. "Don't be cute with me, weirdo."

"I can't help it. God made me this way."

"A weirdo?"

This wasn't quite working but he pressed on. "No. God made me cute."

She huffed and walked out.

Jack scooped ice into his bucket and whistled to himself. She totally wanted him. He should have said something exciting about his injuries, though. Women love the idea of fights and action. And so what if getting whacked in the face and knocked out cold while trying to vomit in a dumpster wasn't exactly a Steven Seagal move? It was certainly more impressive than the "I strained my knee trying to move my desk to the corner of my cubicle" type of move most men have these days. Most men are wussies. *And completely incapable of throwing the leg of a cheap hotel love seat through a man's chest*, he suddenly thought. *Was that part of my hallucination, too?* It seemed really improbable.

His bucket full, Jack turned around to head back to his injured friend and their injured captive... and there she was again, right behind him.

"Listen, buddy," she said. "Watch yourself. I know your game."

He looked at her, not sure what to say. She reached forward and put one of her earbuds next to his right ear. "Hear that?"

Jack heard raucous music playing. He nodded.

"Well, that's what you're headed for," she said.

"I'm headed for being in a rock band?"

"No, the lyrics. Did you not listen to the lyrics?"

Jack shook his head.

"I had it cued up and everything." She frowned at her mp3 player and backed the track up a little. Then she stuck both earbuds into Jack's ears and hit play.

"YOU'RE ON THE HIIIIIIWAY TO HEEEEELLL!" the singer screeched.

"Did you hear it?" she said. Jack pretended he couldn't hear her, pointing at the earbuds and shrugging.

"DID YOU HEAR IT!?" she yelled at him.

Jack still pretended he couldn't hear. She yanked the earbuds from his ears and was about to bellow at him when he said, "I heard, I heard."

"Well, you are," she said. "What the song said, I mean."

"Thanks for the warning."

"So?" she said.

"Yes?"

"Your Asian friend?"

"Yes?"

"He was cuter than you," she said, and she plugged her earbuds back into her ears, spun on her heel and walked away.

Jack laughed, grabbed the ice bucket and headed back to his room.

When he got there, Pak was looking pretty bad. Jack took a washcloth from the bathroom and put some ice in it, then handed it to Pak. Pak put it on the back of his head, then said to Jack, "I need something from you."

"Yes?" Jack said.

"I need some rope."

"Rope?"

"Yes," said Pak. "And a blowtorch."

Jack blinked. "You mean... you're going to..."

Pak continued "And one quart of *Pebblefield Farms* organic yogurt."

"What?"

"Just get it. You can find at expensive grocery stores. Also, see if you can get aspirin from front desk. Get that first, Jack, then get me the rest."

Feeling his own throbbing headache, Jack agreed with this choice, and he headed to the lobby.

✳ ✳ ✳

"How's your buddy?" yelled a businessman in the lobby.

"He's fine," said Jack, "just sleeping it off now."

The businessman snorted. "Well, well, you're a good friend to him. I would've left his sorry carcass to be picked clean by vultures."

"I thought about it," Jack said truthfully. *Or I could have left him in a baseball dugout.*

He rang the bell at the front counter and a young man appeared a moment later. "Yes sir, how may I help you?"

"Aspirin. Do you have aspirin?"

"Yes sir, one moment."

The clerk reached under the counter and came back with a couple of single-serving aspirin packets.

"More?" asked Jack.

The clerk grabbed a handful and put them on the counter. They glowed magnificently.

"And..." Jack decided to try for it, "do you have any *Ocean Octaves!?*"

The man looked at him with a puzzled expression. "No sir, very sorry—I'm not sure what those are."

"Never mind," said Jack, and he walked back to his room.

He got Pak a cup of water and watched as his friend swallowed four tablets. He took a couple himself. The Korean was still out cold. Pak had tied him up with the telephone cord. That telephone was really getting a lot of use, none of which involved its intended one. Jack grabbed his wallet and went downstairs to catch a cab.

The man at the front desk had to call one for him. Jack realized he'd never actually taken a cab before. *Real spy stuff here*, he thought. *Next thing you know I'll be in a night club surrounded by gangsters and femme fatales.*

He waited by the curb for a couple of minutes until the cab showed up. He got in and pulled the door shut. "Where you like to go, sir?" said the driver, in accented English.

"The closest hardware store, please, and wait for me there. I also have to go to a good grocery store. The kind with organic yogurt."

"No problem."

"And *Ocean Octaves!*" Jack added.

Within 45 minutes Jack had collected what Pak needed—plus three bags, three glorious bags of the best seaweed crisps on the planet—then paid the cabbie (man alive—it was expensive to hire a cab) then returned to his room.

The Korean was still knocked out. Jack wondered for a moment if Pak had killed the guy, then noted he was still breathing.

"Get a chair, Jack, then we tie him to it."

Jack grabbed the lacquered wooden chair by the desk in the room.

"Pak...?"

"Not now, Jack. Help me tie him up."

Jack did, feeling somewhat uncomfortable with the turn things were taking. Sure, this Korean guy might be a psychopathic boss-killer, but he was certain there were plenty of boss-killers in the world who didn't need torturing. Some might even deserve medals. He gritted his teeth. *Remember what you swore to Hardin, Jack. Revenge.*

"Jack, do we have matches?"

"I forgot," Jack said. "I'll see if I can get some from the lobby."

Jack ran down the stairs breathlessly. He was really starting to second-guess this spy thing. *Who IS Pak? Maybe he is a total psycho himself, operating for some other evil ring of international gardeners who torture other rival members in their spare time.*

This is a pretty nice place to torture people, though, Jack thought as he looked at the tasteful lobby area. *Usually, people get tortured in warehouses, filthy barns, dungeons, things like that. Not places with good carpet and a faint aroma of cinnamon and vanilla. Of course, the carpet in the room isn't that nice anymore, and the love seat is busted, so maybe–*

Then his chain of thought was interrupted by the man behind the reception desk.

"Matches?" he said.

"Yes, sir," the man said, handing him a book of matches. "There is no smoking in the rooms, however. Designated smoking areas have been provided on each floor, as you'll see by the signs."

"Oh yes, thank you, I did see that," Jack said. He figured it wouldn't be wise to confess he was a non-smoker who just needed the matches to light the blow torch in his room.

Jack raced back upstairs, tired by the time he made it to his floor. He paused outside their room.

Jack... you can walk away right now. You do not have to help Pak torture a Korean. You tried to save your boss. You got ice. You picked up torture supplies from the hardware store. Jack winced at that thought. Was he already a culprit? In for a penny, in for a pound? Could the fuzz bust him for picking up a blowtorch and rope from the hardware store? He imagined the cabbie describing him to the police.

"Yes, officer. Man was maybe five feet, ten inch tall? Bruises on his face."

"Like this guy?" the officer would say, pointing to Jack in a line-up of 5'10"-tall men with bruised faces.

"Ah yes, that one there! Wearing the '*Ocean Octaves!*' promotional giveaway 2013 shirt. He actually bought some of those snacks on the trip—now I remember!"

Then Jack would be taken away to prison for the next few decades, never having a chance to start a little soil lab of his own. *Actually, I don't really want a soil lab,* Jack thought. *But I wouldn't get to see how those turnips turn out. But still—maybe I'm already in this too deeply.*

Jack remembered his vow to Hardin, but it seemed so far off already, a hazy recollection from a past life. But that was just the drug. He had sworn—he knew because Pak remembered. And part of fulfilling that vow meant he needed to be tough. Maybe he could just kill this Korean and be done with it? No, the whole thing went deeper than that.

The Korean was just a tool in some much bigger toolkit. A toolkit of pure evil. And others will die. Will this vengeance thing be an endless chain? But still, I can't help torture him. I don't even like it when I cut through an earthworm in the garden. Then again, throwing that love seat leg was exciting and you don't feel bad about that, do you Jack? *Yeah, but he was yelling at me. And torture? I mean–*

The door swung open from within. Pak nodded and took the matches from Jack's hand. *Which door is this?* thought Jack as he walked in. *Campbell wrote about a door. Am I walking through it now?*

"Jack—he's waking up," Pak said, interrupting his thoughts.

Jack looked over at the Korean. He was gagged with a a washcloth, yet his eyes stared defiantly at the two of them.

He will kill me if he gets away. Or his compatriots will kill me. It's very likely. This is a torture-or-be-tortured world, Jack considered philosophically. When you thought of it that way, you might as well torture.

Pak whispered in Jack's ear. "Listen, Jack—this may be tough for you to watch."

Jack swallowed and nodded.

"Seeing a man panic is tough. Men are supposed to be rocks against which the world beats itself like grey waves on golden shore."

"Yeah, Pak. I guess so."

"Good, good. You take the notebook off the desk and be ready to write notes, okay?"

Jack had read that torture never resulted in reliable information. Maybe it was in *The Sun*, but he hadn't finished the article because a sidebar with a starlet's bikini baby bump distracted him. But he believed it was useless to use torture. But maybe Pak knew something he didn't. Or maybe Pak was a psychopath.

Pak lit the torch, and the Korean's eyes widened.

"Take off his gag, Jack."

Jack took off the gag. The Korean tried to bite him without success. Pak walked closer with the torch. "Tell me why you kidnapped Hardin, why you killed him," he said.

The Korean spat on him. "You can't make me talk."

"Do I write that down, Pak?" Jack asked.

Pak waved him off and took a step closer to his victim.

"You want to bet on my ability to make you talk?"

"Torturing me will reveal nothing. I resist until death. You will learn nothing—nothing!"

"Torture you?" Pak said. "Why, I wouldn't dream of it." He smiled and reached into a brown 100% post-consumer paper bag and pulled out a container. "Ah, what have we here?"

The Korean stared at him, uncertain.

"Yes, yes," Pak said, holding up the container and studying its side. "A picture of a green field. A nice field. With cows." He rotated the container slowly. "Ah, it is some kind of fermented treat. Made from the milk of cows, cultured with a variety of very interesting living creatures."

The Korean went pale.

"Yes, yes—it is something called Pebblefield Farms Organic Full Milkfat Yogurt. And it contains active cultures."

The Korean struggled against his bonds.

"...including Acidophilus," Pak concluded, nodding slowly.

The Korean gasped.

Pak hefted the yogurt in one hand, the lit blowtorch in the other, then he handed the container to Jack. "Open the yogurt, Jack."

Jack complied, completely baffled, terrified of whatever horrible thing was going to happen next. He felt ill inside, but he did what Pak directed, as if his own will had been drained and replaced with the psychotic directives of a crazy Chinaman. He wondered if Pak had been mentally damaged by the multiple hits to his head. It could be. Jack had not really been close friends with Pak before—just decent neighbors and garden enthusiasts—but he could not visualize Pak, this good-humored guy, as being the sort of man who would waterboard a Korean with yogurt while burning off his fingernails with a torch.

It just didn't seem possible.

"Put the yogurt in the bowl, Jack."

"The b-b-bowl?" Jack stammered.

"The bowl. The bowl on the counter containing the complimentary package of oatmeal with trivia questions on the back."

Jack picked up the bowl, taking out the package of oatmeal. Cinnamon and sugar.

"*This period of state-sponsored terror was known as the _____*" he read as he tossed the oatmeal onto the counter.

"Should I wash the bowl first?" he asked Pak, hoping that perhaps he and the Korean were merely about to share an extraordinarily late breakfast.

"Put the yogurt in the bowl, Jack."

Jack complied, pouring it out with a thick plop, then he handed the bowl to Pak, who placed it carefully on top of the little desk.

"Now, my Korean friend, it is time to talk."

The Korean shook his head.

Pak turned the torch higher and started to pass the flame just above the surface of the yogurt.

"You maniac!" the Korean yelped.

Man calls Pak a maniac, Jack wrote.

Pak ignored him and passed the flame closer.

"Billions of lives! It is genocide!" the Korean wailed.

Pak stared at him coldly. Jack kept writing.

"Talk. Tell me why you took Hardin."

"I... can't!" the man said.

Man can't, Jack wrote.

Pak shook his head, wincing again. He looked unsteady on his feet, but managed to stay upright. Jack put a hand on his shoulder.

"You okay, Pak?" he whispered.

"Yes, Jack. Just get me a spoon now."

"A... spoon? You want me to stop writing?"

"For this moment, yes. A spoon."

This was getting really strange. Was Pak going to heat up the yogurt, then drip it on the Korean with a spoon? It sounded really painful. Jack's conscience died a little more as he gave Pak the spoon.

Pak dipped it slowly into the yogurt and took out a spoonful, then raised it up in the air towards the Korean.

"Don't... you... don't!" the Korean whimpered.

Pak slowly brought the torch closer to the spoon of yogurt.

"Entire cultures! Think of it, you monster!" the Korean spat. "Think of it! You would destroy an living cultures!?"

"You are the one destroying them," Pak said, holding the blue tip of the flame beneath the spoon. "You refuse to speak, you condemn them. I am but the tool—you are the instigation."

"FINE!" yelped the Korean. "I took Hardin because he is like you!"

"Like me?" Pak said, pulling the torch back from the spoon.

"Genocidal. Destroyers of life. The tiniest life, the most beautiful, intricate life. You multicellular supremacists are disgusting!"

Pak brought the torch closer to the yogurt again. "I did not ask for insults—I asked for information. You killed Hardin because...?"

"Because he destroys life—soil life! Including fungi!"

Jack frowned. "He helped farmers figure out what they need to add to their soil!"

The Korean laughed bitterly. "Inorganic compounds—like adjusting a pocket watch with a hammer."

Jack wondered if anyone still carried pocket watches, then realized he had failed to write down half the conversation.

"Yes, a hammer. Ignoring the intricate web of microorganisms in every precious teaspoon. Drying, heating, grinding, soaking with chemicals... killing billions! Billions of lives!"

Pak nodded. "This is consistent with their philosophy, Jack."

"Their... what? Really?" Jack said.

The Korean continued, "The size is not what matters in this life. The quantity of lives is incredible—the quantity you ruthlessly destroy just through your life, while calling these tiny creatures names such as 'pestilence', 'disease', 'filth'. You are the filth! Antibiotics—weapons of mass destruction! Hand sanitizer—murder gel!" The Korean was almost sobbing.

Jack noticed that Pak was no longer anywhere near the yogurt with the torch. He wondered if the torture was turning even his stomach.

"Listen, agent," Pak said, "you have been killing people, correct?"

"Killing those who are non-persons through their acts of terror against life!" the Korean shrieked. "Monsters—like you—and YOU!" he jerked his head towards Jack.

Undeterred, Pak continued. "Soil scientists? Professors? Businessmen who work in agriculture?"

"Mass-murderers!"

"But... why take them places for questioning, like you did with Hardin? And what about the drugging? Leaving them in the desert?"

Jack wondered the same thing. The Koreans could have killed Hardin at any point. They could have put something lethal in his meal instead of a hallucinogen.

The Korean stared daggers at Pak. Pak slowly moved the flame towards the yogurt again and the man spoke.

"I drug them, ask questions about their accomplices. So many need judgment upon them. So many—and yet they walk free. One by one, I disrupt and infiltrate their web, even as they disrupt and destroy the sacred web of the soil."

"But why dump them in the wilderness?"

"Because nature—they need to learn what she is really like to those who cross her! She is the one that wreaks the vengeance. Stings of scorpion, bite of hyena, death by drowning, falling, dehydration, exposure, ants, snakes, falling on spiky plants—this is final taste they have of what they themselves have done to the tiniest of life!"

"Makes sense," Pak said. "I am a fan of no-till methods, personally, but Jack here is a digger. Cruel to nature."

"Wait..." Jack said.

"It's okay, Jack—I won't blowtorch your *Ocean Octaves!*"

Jack had a brief vision of himself tied to a chair while Pak roasted bags of *Ocean Octaves!* as he struggled and pleaded. He shuddered. Then had a completely different thought.

"Wait a minute!" he turned to the Korean. "Don't you eat fermented food? Aren't you also a killer?"

The Korean said nothing.

Pak raised an eyebrow. "Good question, Jack. Answer him!"

The Korean sighed. "Yes, of course. I take them into this body. For many millennia we have lived side by side, inside and outside each other. Kimchi organisms colonize and live within man."

"Doesn't the stomach acid kill it?" Jack asked.

"Humans breed them in food, you fool," said the Korean. "They give them perfect environment, balance of salt, plant materials to consume, carbohydrates, good environment and in turn they become part of the human. Not wanton killing, not murderous practice of farmers and sterilizing! Not destruction of cultures, but living in and through them, nurturing and partaking!"

"Don't try to make sense of it, Jack," Pak whispered. "Remember this guy is talking to us because I was going to torch a teaspoon of yogurt."

"That's true," Jack whispered back. "Actually, shouldn't we get more info out of him? Like, maybe a list of people they're going to kill next? I missed some of the previous stuff he said, but I could write that down."

"Yes—good—thank you, Jack. My head hurts—can barely stand right now. I hope you're writing."

"Oh yeah, lots," Jack said, picking the notebook up again.

Pak turned back to the Korean.

"So, what is next? Who are you going to kill?"

(Pak asks who man is going to kill), Jack wrote.

The Korean laughed.

"You! Ha ha! You!"

(Will kill Pak)

"How will you do that? You are tied to a chair."

(But can't tied to chair, Pak says.)

The Korean shrugged.

Jack had a thought. "Wait, Pak—what if they are going to attack here?"

"Attack?" said Pak.

"Well, it's an agricultural convention. Plenty of mass murderers. What if they have some sort of plan?"

"A bomb?" Pak gasped. "That's..."

(I ask about attack on convention. Pak says bomb)

The Korean smiled at them both.

"Is there a bomb?" Pak asked.

The Korean shrugged.

(Man shrugs about bomb)

Pak held the torch close to the teaspoon.

"Answer me!" he ordered his captive.

(Pak threatens man with torch)

The Korean shook his head.

Pak held the flame under the yogurt until it bubbled.

(Pak cooks yogurt)

"I will not!" said the Korean. "If there is no chance I can go free, there is no chance the cultures you are destroying will go free! We will all be incinerated and die together!"

"I think that means there's a bomb," Jack said.

(I say there's a bomb because Korean says all will die)

Pak nodded, then slumped to the floor, the lit torch falling from his hand.

"Head injuries are very dangerous," the Korean said, and laughed. "Very very dangerous," he said again, now cackling like a maniac. "Very, very, very, very..."

And suddenly he stopped. Jack had hit him in the head with the now extinguished blow torch.

Jack ran to help Pak to his feet.

"Pak... are you awake?"

Pak's eyes were rolling inside his head. Quickly, Jack laid his friend out on the bed, surprised that such a small fellow was still such a pain to move about.

He then gagged the Korean in case he woke up. He wondered if there was a chance the guy would suffocate just trying to breathe through his nose, then decided he didn't care.

CHAPTER TWELVE

Jack picked up Pak's limp form, left the room and took the elevator down to the lobby.

"Another drunk?" said the fat businessman as Jack walked through with Pak over his shoulder.

Jack ignored the man and headed for the parking lot. There—the cab was still there! He waved to the driver.

"Sir?" the man asked.

"Would you drive us to the hospital?" Jack asked. "My friend here has a head injury."

"Good sir, yes sir. Which hospital?"

"Which hospital kills the least patients?"

The driver thought for a moment. "Well, Thomas Pike is good. Highly rated ER. But they're probably better on the cardiovascular side than they are on head injuries."

"Okay," Jack said, "so...?"

"And you don't want to go to Cooper. They'll kill him. My cousin went in there with a broken toe and left with hepatitis and diabetes."

"Really?"

"St. Agatha's isn't bad. Though the stitches tore the first day for my sister. I think they were using low-test fishing line. Yet they do CT scans. You know, on brains. Great color on the images."

"But are they actually good?"

"Oh yeah, pictures are great. Almost 3D. Another option is Celestial Valley Hospital. Nice place, good interior design. Leads the area in kidney transplants."

"My friend doesn't need a kidney."

"Not that he knows of," said the cabbie. "You often don't know about those sorts of things until it's too late."

"Look—it's going to be too late if we don't get him to a hospital for this head injury!"

"Right, right. So which hospital, boss?"

"Just go to the closest one!" Jack ordered, deciding that any hospital was probably better than none. Pak was slumped awkwardly in the seat next to him. Jack didn't feel well himself. He felt a burning need deep inside him for *Ocean Octaves!* He cursed himself for leaving them back in the room. What with the torturing and bosses dying and friends collapsing and all, it was hard to focus on the important stuff. Self-care, he remembered hearing it called. *Ocean Octaves!* were part of self-care.

They reached St. Paisley's Medical Hospital in a few minutes. Jack paid the cabbie and unloaded Pak at the emergency room.

"Nurse?" he said to the woman behind the front desk. She held up a finger. Three other people were in front of Jack, apparently filling out paperwork or waiting to do so. The waiting room had another dozen people in it. One woman was wearing plastic trash bags and tape. Across from her, an old man was hunched over with his fingers in his ears. A mother had a sleeping child on her lap. A one-legged man was working on the lacing securing his prosthetic limb. Another young couple held hands. The male half of the couple twitched and shifted his gaze here and there about the room, obviously on some sort of drugs.

"Nurse," Jack pressed, "he got hit on the head—badly—and passed out."

She looked up. "You look like you got hit on the head as well."

"I'm okay," Jack said, "but he's a mess." She looked at Pak as he lay slumped on the chair beside Jack.

"Drunk?" she asked.

Jack shook his head. "No. I told you. Head injury."

"Oh, right. Head injuries can be very bad," she said, then called back to someone behind her.

A moment later, a short and muscular Hispanic man rounded the corner through the double doors with a wheelchair.

"This your friend?" he asked.

Jack nodded.

"Follow me."

He expertly loaded Pak into the wheelchair, making it look easy. *I'll bet this guy has to move people all day. The female nurses probably make him do the heavy lifting.* Then another thought came to him. *I'll bet this guy carries dead people down to the morgue, too.* He imagined the guy with a corpse over each shoulder, trailing tubes and wires behind them, marching down a greenly lit corridor, down to a creepy room filled with waxy-faced morticians pumping embalming fluid into expired bakers, grandmothers, golfers, gangsters, and...

"We need you to fill out some paperwork, alright?" said the man, interrupting Jack's thoughts. They had reached a nurse's station in another wing.

He left Jack at the desk and wheeled Pak off into the antiseptic bowels of the hospital. The nurse behind the desk looked up at Jack.

"Relation to the patient?" she asked.

"Friend," Jack answered. He was pretty sure he was Pak's friend, especially since Pak didn't actually torch people tied to chairs in hotels. At least, he hadn't this time. Yes, friend worked.

"Occupation?"

"Me or Pak?" Jack asked.

"Meatpack?" she said. "Meatpacking?"

"No, no—I said 'Me or Pak.' My friend's name is Pak."

"First or last name?"

"Last name is Choi. First name, Pak."

"Pak Choi? Really?"

"Yes—that's right."

She rolled her eyes. "That's a vegetable. Is your friend a vegetable?"

Jack frowned at her. "Well, I suppose that depends on the level of care you give him."

"Fair enough," she said. "Your name?"

"Broccoli. Jack Broccoli."

"Oh nice, that's real cute. Pak Choi and Jack Broccoli. Do you do gigs at the local vegan restaurant?"

"Please, nurse... I really need to get going."

"Get going? I don't think so. You need to fill out all of these properly," she clipped a thick stack of papers to a clipboard, then pushed them across the counter to Jack.

"And then I can go?"

She shook her head. "No. Then you need to speak with the police."

A tinge of fear tickled Jack's spine. "The police?"

"Duh, yes. You drag a guy in here, unconscious, with head injuries? There's going to be an inquest."

Jack shook his head. It still hurt when he did that. He made a note not to do it anymore, remembering that Pak had just passed out from a head injury. He put his hand to his head as he tried again with the nurse.

"Look, I was injured too. I don't have time for this—I need to get back to the hotel. It's very important."

"Ah, right. You're here for the anime convention?"

"The?"

"Anime convention? Figures. You should see some of the cosplay injuries we get. Some of them are hilarious. Actually, I shouldn't show you this, but..."

She took an x-ray print from under the desk and slipped it to Jack. "Isn't that a hoot?" she said.

Jack couldn't make out what was happening. It looked like a gigantic axe was lodged in... that couldn't be right.

He fake-laughed at the nurse. "Wow, that is a hoot."

She nodded. "And look at this one!"

She passed him a photo of a person whose jaw had been wired shut. It looked horrid.

"Hit in the mouth with a giant fake sword. Made of wood."

"Wood?"

"Yeah. Kid made it at home. Lots of splinters. Spray-painted silver. Took forever to get all the splinters out of that girl's face."

"Girl?" Jack asked, looking at the photo. The face was almost completely round and puffy with fat. Sex was impossible to distinguish. He wondered if wiring the girl's jaw shut might actually help her lose some weight. One of those clickbait stories: "I was hit in the face and it turned my life around."

"You really do get some hard work around here—my hat is off," Jack said, hoping the nurse would just let him go.

"Ha!" she said. "You don't know the half of it! Ever seen what happens when you botch a catheter on a 300 lb achondroplastic dwarf?"

Jack blinked and the nurse continued. "Yep. Their knees can't take their weight when they eat junk all day. Blow up like little balloons. Then can't pee. Terrible."

Jack was pretty sure this wasn't a politically correct thing to say about Calorically Abundant Little-Americans, or whatever the proper term was for congenitally short, highly weighted individuals.

"Nurse, is there a restroom?"

She nodded. "Right over there, unless you'd rather be catheterized."

"No, thank you," Jack said, wincing, as he walked away towards the bathroom.

I have to figure out how to get out of here. Lives hang in the balance.

The bathroom was white and green with that clinical hospital cleanliness and a faint odor of something harsh and chemical. Jack wracked his brain. It already hurt from the day's activities and beatings.

He felt that the nurse was warming up to him, but he didn't think she was going to just let him waltz out the door without calling the authorities on him. Any minute, an officer might come in. He didn't know if one had been called or not, never having been in such a peculiar position. He needed to build rapport with her. Women always loved him, and this one should be no different. Yet she was also quite professional. He needed to walk a tightrope.

There must be a special line to take with nurses. They're certainly not normal.

He remembered a nurse friend of his mother's from when he was a boy. She lived on Snickers bars, Diet Coke and Virginia Slims and told stories that made your eyelids peel. Why health professionals ate the diets they did, Jack had no idea.

He pulled out his phone and DuckDuckGoed "making a nurse like you". After finding nothing useful except for a bizarre DIY article demonstrating how to mold a self-portrait in scrubs from polymer clay, he decided he needed to work it out for himself.

Let's see... what do nurses like?

He started to make a list on his phone's note pad:

Nurses Like:

- Virginia Slims

- Diet Coke (other sodas too?)

- Snickers Bars (other chocolates too?)

- Horrible Medical Stories

That really was all he could think of. He also knew most people liked talking about themselves. The nurse had already told him one gross work story, so that was definitely a "like" of hers. But could he build a fast camaraderie with her in time to escape and make it back to the convention?

He had to try. He was now an international man of mystery—well, a national one at least, but Pak was from another country so that kind of gave him a leg up—and he couldn't be bothered to wait around for the authorities to show up and waste his time while scary guys blew up a bunch of his agricultural colleagues. His time was now—and he had to be the suavest, most charming, most desirable Jack Broccoli he could be.

This would be easy.

Jack looked in the mirror and smoothed his hair with some water from the sink. His face didn't look very good with the bruise and the Band-Aid, but it made him look roguish. Women loved psychotic criminals, he'd once read, so perhaps it would help. Of course, he thought, peering at his face closer, he might look rather more like a victim. He didn't have that scary look to his face. It was boyish, really. He wondered if he had time to draw a tattoo on his arm. Maybe a bikini-clad woman being dragged into the flames by a skeleton in an SS uniform? No, definitely don't have the time for that. Or the drawing ability. Or a pen, come to think of it.

No, he just needed to start with what he knew nurses loved, then roll with that. He grinned to himself, then threw open the door and walked confidently back towards the nurse at the counter.

Before he could say anything she smirked at him. "You need a laxative?"

Jack laughed it off. "No, thank you," said Jack, "I've got great moves as it is."

He couldn't believe he just said that.

She cocked an eyebrow at him. Despite being a nurse—which automatically made her terrifying—she wasn't a bad-looking gal. Maybe 30-something? Mouth was a little hard and her hair was pulled back into a severe bun, but she really looked less scary than his mom's old friend.

"Take a seat, the police should be here soon," she said.

Jack's heart jumped inside him. That wasn't good. They had called them.

"Thank you, nurse. Nurse...?"

"Allen."

"Allen is your name? Is that short for Allenette?"

"No, it's my last name."

"Likely story," Jack said.

She was looking at something on her computer screen.

"Catheters?" he said.

"What?" she said, looking up.

"Dwarf catheters."

"Ah, you liked that?"

"Yeah," Jack lied. "Reminds me of picking off scabs."

"Oooh... I love doing that," she said, looking more intently at him.

Jack pressed onwards. "Yes, it's great. I used to pick at them all the time when I was a kid."

"I still like picking at them," she said.

"Mmmhmm. I like the really, really long ones you can peel slowly." said Jack.

Her pupils dilated as she leaned towards him. "Oh yes. And the infected ones."

Jack almost winced but kept his face steely. "Yes, those are great to pick. But you sound like you really get into it. You ride a bike or something, so you get scabs often?"

He knew nurses didn't ride bikes. *Why did he say that?*

"No, no," she laughed. "I like to pick other people's scabs."

Jack was pretty sure his stomach had just thrown up inside his stomach, but he recovered suavely and made a cocky, half-grin.

"Listen, Nurse Allen—why don't you get us a couple of cokes? You can make yours diet."

"How did you know I liked Diet Coke?" she replied.

Jack shrugged. "I just knew."

"There's a machine in the hallway," she said, rooting in her purse and handing him a bill. "Go grab them then come back. Lounge is right there. Hurry up—I want to tell you a scab story that will burn the hair off your ears."

"I can't wait," said Jack with a wink, then stepped through a pair of double doors into a little lounge area. It was the wrong direction, but he had to get that Diet Coke.

Brilliant, he thought, noticing there was also a snack machine with Snickers bars. He was going to trust his gut on this one. Diet Coke and a Snickers.

Holy moly... Snickers bars are $2.59 here. That is insane. In an era of mostly socialized medicine, he found this a grave injustice. Didn't the government have penalties against price-gouging? Had no progressive senator thought "Hey, let's make candy in hospitals cheaper for needy nurse-chasers?" Apparently not.

He clenched his teeth with an intake of breath as he looked at the paper money intake slot on the machine. It leered back at him with its hungry, bill-eating mouth.

With trembling hands, he took the bill the nurse had handed him—a five, darn her, that would barely cover her soda, let alone his—and fed it into the machine, insuring that Lincoln's mournful face was right side up.

Lincoln disappeared smoothly.

For a moment, it looked as if the president had fulfilled his mission. Then he came back out again. Jack thought an ungracious thought about theaters and carefully fed the bill back in. This time, it stayed.

He punched his selection and the little curlicue spring unwound and the Snickers bar fell into the dispensing slot.

"Yes!" he said, perhaps too loudly, and snagged it. He imagined taking it to Nurse Allen and suavely saying, "Not going anywhere for a while?" *No, don't say that Jack. It's too stupid.*

But before he got back to the nurse, he had to complete the same maneuver with the soda machine. Stepping in front of it, he thought he knew what it was like to step into the ring with Mike Tyson. This had to work. The Diet Cokes were $3.50 each. Ouch. Then he had a sickening realization.

No... it can't be... Yes, it is.

It was the same model machine that had beaten him at the office. Well, he'd beaten it, but this was no time to mince words. Jack said a little prayer, opened his wallet and took out a ten, then pressed it into the slot and watched Hamilton disappear. If anyone had a chance of getting a Diet Coke for him, it would have to be Hamilton, father of the first US Central Bank.

After a long and terrifying pause, the bill came slightly back out and jammed in the slot.

No! No, it can't be!

He tried pulling at the now ripped edge of the bill but it was stuck. "Come on... come on," he muttered. He pulled a little harder and it suddenly unspooled from the slot.

He flattened the bill, pulling it across the corner of the machine to make sure it was as flat as he could make it, then knocked on a little wood table, crossed his finger, and threw a pinch of imaginary salt over his shoulder. Then he put the bill back into the machine. Hamilton disappeared and stayed gone.

He punched in the number for Diet Coke. The machine started to dispense the drink, then stopped. The coke was hanging right at the edge.

Unbelievable! No, this couldn't be! Not now! Not when this very important man of international mystery superspy was about to pull a *coup d'état* and get a nurse all goggly eyed over his suave handsomeness just in time to defuse a bomb! No! He would not be foiled by a machine!

He gave the machine a tiny push. The Diet Coke shook slightly but failed to move any closer to the precipice that stood between Jack and salvation.

He pushed a little harder.

Nothing.

He looked around and back through the windows of the double-door. No one was coming, so he grabbed the front of the machine with both hands and tried tilting it towards him. It was heavy. *Are they bolting these things to the floor now? Have angry cancer patients been coming in here and jostling soda machines?*

Jack pulled harder and the machine started to move forward just a little, then banged back as his feet slipped on the linoleum floor. He grabbed again, tighter, and tried again. No luck.

Maybe if I push forward and rock back again? He tried that, shoving the front of the machine, then pulling back, then pushing forward. He started to get a rhythm going. The Diet Coke was moving forwards—it was happening—so close!

Thump, rock, thump, rock, thump, rockety rockety thump!

Then the doors opened, surprising Jack and causing him to suddenly let go.

THWACK! The machine hit the ground hard, falling back from an almost 25-degree angle.

"What's going on here?" said a frowning police officer.

"I just..." Jack spluttered lamely.

The officer's frown deepened.

"Vandalism?"

"No, I'm just trying to get a..."

THUMP! The Diet Coke fell into the slot.

Jack grabbed it coolly. "Diet Coke."

The officer was joined by another who was also frowning. The second officer had his hand on his gun. Jack wondered why the government hadn't also passed a law disarming belligerent police officers in hospitals.

"I don't trust men who drink Diet Coke," said the first officer.

"It's not for me," said Jack.

"Uh-huh," said the cop. "So, you the guy that beat up the Asian fellow?"

"Beat up?" Jack said. "No."

"Right," the officer continued. "Sure, you're just a Good Samaritan who picked up a wounded guy on the street and decided to bring him in."

"He wasn't on the street."

"So you beat him up in his house?" the officer said.

"Don't I have the right to remain silent or something?" said Jack, realizing that this wasn't really going well.

The cop rolled his eyes. "Well, if you say so, I can read you your rights, then arrest you."

"No," Jack said. "I'd rather not." Then he had a thought. "Hey officer... here."

He handed the officer a Snickers bar.

The officer waved him off. "So, assault, then vandalism, then bribing an officer?"

Jack shook his head, "No, no, I just..."

"Not going anywhere for a while?" said officer #2. Both of them sniggered at Jack. Or "snickered," as the case might be.

Jack was very glad he'd rejected that line. It really did sound stupid.

And meanwhile, as the cop made an obvious joke, hundreds of agriculturalists, suppliers and salesmen were about to be blown up. The last group might not be much of a loss, but he was rather fond of certain members of the first two groups. This wasn't turning out to be his lucky day.

He had a choice. Go with the officers, or...

As the officers snickered, he made his decision and set off at a run.

Unfortunately, officer #2 was ready and kicked out his leg, tangling up Jack's feet and sending him sprawling. The Diet Coke rolled across the floor, dented by the impact but still intact.

Officer #1 had his taser ready, Officer #2 pulled his gun.

"DOWN! STAY DOWN!" one of them yelled.

EVERYTHING IS A WEAPON, said the voice in Jack's head.

"You want me to fight the police?" Jack said under his breath.

YOU ARE THE CARETAKER—YOU MUST ESCAPE.

"Great," said Jack, "why not."

One of the officers was now on Jack's back, clutching at his arms and trying to force his hands into cuffs. He rolled over, throwing the officer off onto the ground. The man fell hard—but as Jack jumped to his feet, a jolt of pain shook his body—he was being tasered! He staggered to the ground as the officer with the gun regained his feet. Both of them were over him, raining blows and kicks into him.

EVERYTHING IS A WEAPON!!!

Lashing out with his arm, Jack grabbed the end of one of the officer's slacks and yanked. The pants ripped away from the man's legs like paper. Both officers jumped back as he leapt to his feet, twirling the pants like the rotor of a helicopter. Faster and faster he spun them until they whistled through the air. Jack had no idea he could spin something so quickly—then he realized his newfound powers were with him.

"As soon as I drop these pants, they'll be on me."

He didn't want to kill the cops. That would be bad. But he did need them to leave him alone.

Cop #2 had his gun out! With a zip of his wrist, Jack caught it with the spinning pants, shearing off the end of the barrel. The man's arm jerked to the side with a cracking sound and he went down yelling and clutching his shoulder. The pantsless officer put his hands up as Jack walked towards him, the whirling edge of the pants like a vengeful blade of death over his head.

"Look, man—look—we're adults here!" said the officer, looking ridiculous in his underpants.

The circling pants were now smoking. Jack wondered what he should do next. The officer with the injured shoulder was pressed back against the wall, eyeing the door—but Jack was in the way.

As soon as I drop these pants, they'll be on me.

He decided to back out the door while twirling the pants, but his plan was literally torched by the pants bursting into flame with an explosive WHOOSH!

He threw the disintegrating fabric, and before the cops could respond Jack grabbed the Diet Coke from the floor and ran from the room. He flew past Nurse Allen—who was now flanked by a couple other nervous-looking nurses and a security guy—and tossed the soda to her. She completely failed to catch it and it hit the floor yet again, this time exploding in a spray of foam.

It's the thought that counts he thought, listening to her swear at him as he blew through the doors into the main hallway.

The cops didn't have a chance. He ran past the elevators and down the stars, the door above him banging open as he reached the bottom and ran onto the first floor. He slammed into a ragged man wearing a puppet on his arm as he careened through the ER waiting room. The puppet said something rude but the man's lips didn't move. *Let it go, Jack*, he thought, but he punched the puppet just for spite before continuing his sprint.

Then, just as he passed through the front sliding glass door, an alarm sounded inside the hospital. He raced into the parking lot. In front of the ER, an old woman was helping an even older woman into a wheelchair next to a running minivan with the doors open.

THERE'S YOUR CAR, JACK.

"There's your carjack indeed," Jack muttered, jumping into the van and screeching away from the two women with a "Sorry!" thrown out the window. Their shocked faces hurt him, but he was doing this for the greater good.

How many times can you tell yourself that, Jack?

No time to worry about it. Another cop car was pulling into the parking lot. Jack drove down the ramp, out of the parking lot, off to the hotel.

He drove crazier than he'd ever driven. Jack had always been a very good driver, except for one incident with an old lady and her shopping cart. But he had replaced her groceries, even though it cost him a week's work. Who would have thought a gal like her would have so many snow crab legs? It really was silly, and they shouldn't have scattered all over like that. Packaging just wasn't what it used to be, and he'd only been going about 45. At least he hadn't hit her—and taking a cart around a blind corner like that was ridiculous, especially when there might be distracted drivers trying to sync the MP3 collections on their phone to their new Bluetooth stereos.

Jack took random turns through the parking lots of medical-related businesses around the hospital, then through a neighborhood of town-homes, then back onto the highway. With a sigh of relief, he saw that the cops had failed to tail him. He was pretty sure they'd seen his car, though and hoped they hadn't been able to read the license plate. At least it was stolen, so they couldn't track it to him.

Of course, it was only a matter of time before they went through Pak's wallet, found his identification, tracked his flight, tracked down the hotel reservation, and nailed Jack. Somehow. He knew they could do it. He had no doubt that modern law enforcement could catch anyone. *Maybe they are already tracking my phone.* For a moment he thought about throwing it out of the window, then decided he really couldn't afford that.

Another craving hit him. He needed some *Ocean Octaves!* Bad.

Finally, he reached the hotel. *If they spot the van here, I'm dead,* he thought—then he realized that if the hotel was going to blow up soon, one car in the lot would be a lot less interesting than the flaming shell of a building filled with dead agricultural businessmen. Mind made up, he gave his car to the chauffeur to park.

CHAPTER THIRTEEN

A moment of indecision struck Jack as he walked into the hotel lobby. How would he find out where the bomb was? Should he torture the Korean some more? Did they even have enough yogurt for that?

Call the bomb squad. Are they in the phone book? In the Bs, maybe? Bombs, Making and Supplies; Bombs—Movies, Books and Games; Bombs—Squads and Diffusing (see "Short-Term Employment").

Tell the police? No—definitely not. He pictured the pantsless officer. Which was actually pretty funny, thinking back on it.

Jack walked through the lobby to the stairs. On the way up, he passed the girl. Yes, that girl. She glanced at him for a moment and kept walking. She looked like her mind was somewhere else. He watched her go down the stairs. As she did, he noticed she was looking up and down and around.

Wait a minute...

"Hey," Jack said. Startled, she rounded on him.

"Oh, hey," she said, smiling slightly. "I'd love to talk, but I'm a bit short on time."

"Yeah, me too."

"Why? More palms to bother?"

"*Acacea* need love too."

She pushed open the door, and Jack tried one last tack.

"What are you looking for?"

She turned slowly. "Why do you ask?"

"The way you looked up and down and around."

"It's nothing."

"Are you sure?" Jack said, his words pregnant with meaning. "Are you sure it's not something? Something very, very dangerous?"

Her eyes narrowed. "So... you're the creep who's going to..." She didn't finish her sentence.

"No, not me... I'm not going to..." Jack looked around.

"But..."

"No, I'm..."

"By yourself?" she said.

"I was..."

"But you're not the..."

Jack didn't know how to shake his head no and trail off in the middle, so he just shook his head normally.

"I'm in way over my head," she said. "I have no idea how to find this..."

"Me either," said Jack, "but I think you and I are on the same team."

"What about your Asian friend?" she asked.

"He's Chinese," said Jack.

"Chinese friend."

"Because Russians are Asians too."

"Right," she said. "I forget that."

"It's common," said Jack. "But when you have Asian friends like I do, you learn there are Asians and Asians."

She shook her head impatiently, making her hair bounce in an adorable way. "Where is he? Your Chinese friend?"

"In the hospital," said Jack.

"That's too bad," she said. "I hope he's okay."

Jack nodded. "Yes, me too. But we don't have time to worry right now. We need to save everyone here from being blown up."

"BLOWN UP?" she said. "No way!"

"Yes, by the bomb we're looking for!"

"BOMB!?" she said. "Who said anything about a bomb???"

"Well... I thought you?"

"Oh no. Oh no, not at all! I was looking for my–"

There was a meow from under the stairs. She gasped. "There you are!"

"Wait. You were looking for your cat?" Jack said.

"Dinglebat. I snuck him in."

"Sneaked him in," Jack said, at a loss for words.

"Oh forget that—he's safe! Tell me about this bomb."

Jack was suddenly tongue-tied. His mouth opened, then shut, then opened.

"Are you a crazy bomber?" she asked suddenly, suspicion in her eyes. "If you are, I'm going to scream!"

"No," said Jack, "I am..."

An International Gardening Superspy? A National Gardening Spy? The Incredible Man Who Gets Way Too Many Injuries?

"I'm just this guy, you know?"

"Ha!" she said, "Zaphod!"

Jack grinned. Great, she was a nerd. He could pretend to be a nerd too, to—literally—defuse the situation.

"Right, I'm cos-playing."

"Excuse me?"

Oh, shoot, wrong type of nerd. "I'm creating a scenario for my writing group."

"Writing group?"

"Right. I'm a writer, writing a story about a bomb threat and trying to walk right through it. You like to read, right?"

"No," she said.

"But you recognized my *Hitchhiker's Guide to the Galaxy* quote."

"I saw the movie."

"Ah, right!" Jack was getting warmer now. "Well, my writing group is a... film-writing group!"

"That's neat," she said. "So there isn't really a bomb?"

This was the moment of truth. Or lie. Jack leaned toward making it the moment of lie, but he liked this girl and didn't want her to get blown up.

"Well," Jack said. "It's complicated."

Her cat cocked a suspicious eye at him.

"Well you see... there's this Korean..."

She looked at him blankly, and Jack decided to tell the truth.

"I am here, with my friend, to counter the threat of an international gang of fanatical Korean communists who have been kidnapping, drugging and killing men with careers in the field of agriculture. My friend is currently in the hospital because of head injuries sustained in the course of duty, and I have learned that somewhere in this hotel a bomb is ticking away which eventually is going to kill everyone on the premises, and I don't dare tell the police because I have been told that if I do the Koreans will blow the bomb up immediately and kill everyone, so my only hope is to hunt the bomb down myself before it blows, and I have no idea how to even find a bomb because my day job is being a soil analyst."

Jack took a breath.

The woman leaned in toward him, and she whispered, "You are not alone."

"What?"

"I'm not a bomb tech either, but I am also hunting down the threat. Fortunately, I have a secret weapon."

She nodded to her cat. Jack could've sworn it winked at him.

"Your kitten?"

"Yes," she said. "Dinglebat. My kitten."

"A secret weapon? What, did someone implant a laser in it? Is it a rocket cat? A genetically modified licking machine with a razor-sharp cybernetic tongue?"

"Don't be ridiculous," she sniffed. "This isn't an episode of *Inspector Gadget*. He doesn't have lasers or rockets. He's a bomb-sniffing cat."

"He's a what?"

"A bomb-sniffing cat."

"That's insane," Jack said dismissively. "He's just a kitten."

"That's because of the temporal field."

"Ah," Jack replied, not knowing what else to say. He repeated it. "Ah."

"By the way, what was your name again?" she asked.

"Jack."

"Nice to meet you, Jack. I'm Penny."

Jack laughed involuntarily and she frowned at him.

"You must know," he said.

"Know what?"

"The show. Penny, from the show."

"What show?"

"Oh, never mind," Jack said. "We need to find that bomb."

"Agreed," she said. "I was searching the halls and stairwells first but it could really be anywhere. Dinglebat's nose is only so sensitive."

Jack had an idea. "Penny—maybe we need to think differently."

"Okay," she said. "How?"

"We need to get inside the minds of these people."

"Right, but how do you get inside their minds?"

"Well, let's just free-associate for a bit."

"How do you do that?" Penny asked.

"You just come up with an idea, then follow it with the next idea that comes to mind. I'll start."

"Okay," she replied, sounding dubious.

"Kimchi," he said.

"What's kimchi?" Penny said.

"No, that's not how you do it," Jack said. "Just... come up with something. And it's like sauerkraut."

"Rotten cabbage?"

"Are you giving me an idea or are you referring to sauerkraut?"

"Meow," Dinglebat added.

"Sauerkraut," she said.

"Okay, I'll just count that as your idea after kimchi. Yogurt."

"Why did you say yogurt?" she asked.

"This is how you do free-association," Jack said. It had worked lot better in his tenth grade creative writing class.

"Okay," she said, "but I think this is a waste of time."

"Time," Jack said.

"Oregano," she replied.

"Hey, that's good," Jack said. "You're getting it. Okay, uh, spatula."

"Spatula? That's out of left field!"

"Left-wing," said Jack, not allowing himself to get de-railed.

"Redwing," said Penny.

"Eagle," said Jack.

"Beagle" said Penny.

"Bagel," said Jack, now starting to think this conversation was getting derailed.

"Meow," Dinglebat added again.

"Kung-pow!" said Penny. She was getting into it now.

"Kung-pow?" said Jack, "Did you actually watch that? It was terrible."

"Don't get off track!"

"Right, uh, salad shooter."

"Lee Harvey Oswald."

"Half-dollar."

"Sand-dollar."

"Meow!"

Something in the cat's tone made them both look at him. He was staring back. Had he scented something?

"Simon and Garfunkel," Jack said.

"Lame," said Penny.

"Really? You don't like them? 'Parsley... sage... rosemary... and thyme!' " he sang sensually.

"No. Thyme!"

"Time?"

"No, thyme! Herbs have come up twice now. Maybe we're getting an idea there from the collective unconscious."

"Pak is unconscious. Maybe he sent us the idea. Or maybe you just want me to ask you out to dinner," Jack said.

"The bomb, Jack! The bomb! Maybe it's in the spice cabinet!?"

"The—wait? What? Do they have spice cabinets in hotels? I know this one has real coffee for the coffee makers in the rooms instead of instant, or worse, a boiling pot of aluminum-laced cheap stuff in the lobby with your continental breakfast, but a spice cabinet? There wasn't one in our room. Of course, we were kind of busy torturing that guy. I mean, torturing yogurt."

"No! In the kitchen, Jack!"

"The kitchen? Ah—the main one! Where they make the French toast!"

"Right!" she said.

"Meow," said Dinglebat.

"To the kitchen," said Jack.

* * *

Getting to the kitchen wasn't as easy as Jack had thought. The evening awards ceremony was now in full swing. It was a sit-down dinner with a lot of boring talks, so far as he could figure out. He decided to walk through the back as he was reasonably sure the main kitchen was on the other side. Penny was behind him, Dinglebat in her capacious purse.

He was halfway across the back when he heard a familiar voice calling, "Jack!"

He looked around and saw a tubby man waving at him and walking over. He couldn't place the face for a moment.

"Jack—it's me, Bobby. Bobby Parker!"

"Ah, right," Jack said, realizing suddenly how terrible he looked with his beat-up face and rumpled clothing.

Bobby was the sales guy for a chemical distribution company that supplied AgriTweak. Jack had only met him in person once but had spoken with him on the phone quite a few times. Bobby liked to talk.

"So, my friend, how's the work at AgriTwerk?"

"AgriTweak."

"Yep, yep—what you seek's at AgriTweak! Great, great. Where's Boss Hardin tonight, Jack?"

At the baseball diamond, Jack thought, but didn't say. He shrugged instead. Penny stood behind him, nervously searching around the room with her eyes.

"Ah-ha, ah-ha, a lovely lady here!" Bob said. "Jack, you haven't introduced me to your friend, now have you?"

"No, Bob. Sorry. This is Penny."

"Penny, Penny. Well, well, nice to meet you, Bob's the name, chemicals my game!"

"Right. Bob—I need to keep moving," Jack said.

"Really, really? Well, I see they're just getting started up front here, why don't you sit with me and see what you can see!"

A man was approaching the podium. The lights dimmed and there was a round of applause as the two screens behind the man displayed: "Andy Agnew, President, Agricultural Business Association," with a photo which had obviously been taken a few years before when Andy was thinner and had darker hair.

Jack noted that Andy had a halo and shook his head. He didn't need any more of that—not right now.

"Agriculture," Andy announced, and he waited for the crowd to go completely silent. "Agriculture," he said again, slowly and powerfully. "Agriculture is the soil."

That is true, Jack thought, edging away from Bob, who was watching Andy. He patted the salesman on the shoulder and headed away as fast as he could before Bob could call him back.

Andy droned on. "Agriculture is man—or woman—and sunlight and growing things and bringing good things to eat, growing them from nothing into something, to plates all across America and the world, to exports, and food relief. From laboratories to feedlots, from a young girl with a dream to an old man with a ranch, from a..."

Even if there wasn't a bomb somewhere, Jack would have been racing out. He hated speeches, especially inspirational ones. Penny was right behind him. They made their way carefully along the back of the dim convention hall and passed out into another hallway.

"Jack—if we're wrong," Penny said. "If we're wrong about the herbs..."

"We could be," Jack admitted. "It was just a free association game. It's not like we have some sort of divine guidance."

ACTUALLY, said the steroid voice, startling Jack. He looked at Penny. She obviously hadn't heard it.

"Would you speak softer?" he muttered under his breath.

SORRY. It was still quite loud.

"Divine guidance," Jack muttered. "That's good to know. More like guidance from some sort of split personality in my head..."

"Are you talking to me?" Penny said.

"No—talking to the voice in my head," said Jack. Penny nodded as if that had been a reasonable explanation.

After a few turns, they finally stood outside the "Employees Only" door by the kitchen. Only a few hotel workers were inside. They needed to get in there to search the spice cabinet but neither Penny nor Jack had the slightest idea how to create a ruse that would work to that end. You can't just say, "Hi Chef, mind if I search your spice cabinet for a bomb?"

"What's the plan?" said Penny.

Jack thought for a moment, then spoke. "We'll wait for a cook or server to come out, then crack them over the head and steal their uniform."

"Wow, that's violent," said Penny.

"You stay back. I'll do it," Jack said grimly. "A lot of other heads have gotten cracked today. It's just kind of become a thing."

A moment later, along came a waitress, perhaps fifty, with her salt-and-pepper hair in a bun. She was whistling.

Jack quickly walked up behind her with his hand out, karate-chop style, but he couldn't bring himself to whack her. He didn't want Penny to know that, though, so he pretended to trip and swooshed his hand through the air as he did so, just missing the woman's neck.

"Whoa, there, honey—watch your step!" the waitress said, standing in the door to the kitchen, one hand holding the door. "Can I help you with anything?" she asked, seeing Penny as well.

"Uh, no," said Jack. "Nope, we're fine," said Penny. "Meow," said Dinglebat.

"Meow?" said the waitress.

As she said it, a little ball of fur flew past her feet into the kitchen.

"Well, I'll be darned!" she said. "There aren't supposed to be any cats in the hotel."

"I'm sorry," said Penny. "Let me get him."

The waitress shrugged and waved them into the kitchen. "Come on through. Just don't let management catch you releasing animals into here. The health inspector will shut us down."

"Toxoplasmosis," said Jack. "Makes cat ladies crazy."

Penny frowned at him. "I wasn't the one about to karate chop an innocent waitress," she said under her breath as they walked into the kitchen. There was no sign of Dinglebat.

"Anyone see a cat?" asked the waitress.

"Not I," said the cook as he fried a huge spread of hamburger patties. Jack was impressed—they were the good ones. The pre-made kind that looked like they weren't pre-made. Probably less than 25% TVP. He was suddenly hungry.

"Where's your spice cabinet?" asked Penny.

"What?" said the cook. "Why do you need my spice cabinet?"

"The cat. He might be in there."

"Why would he be in my spice cabinet?"

"Catnip," said Jack.

"I don't have catnip in my spice cabinet," said the cook. "That would be a stupid thing to put in a spice cabinet. This isn't a pet hotel, buddy."

"Sure," said Jack, "but you know, catnip is a type of mint. Good for sore throats and colds. Not just cats."

"Yeah, well I'm not an alternative health doctor either, bud. I'm a cook."

"Just tell me where it is," said Jack.

The cook jerked a thumb to a cabinet nearby.

"It's there, but no cat could get up in there."

"This is a cybernetic laser cat," said Jack.

Penny giggled. She was already opening the cabinet, slowly and carefully.

"What—you afraid the pepper's gonna jump up your nose, lady?" said the cook.

Penny inched the door open. Nothing exploded. Inside were canisters of spices. Garlic powder, onion powder, pepper, rosemary.

"There's no thyme!" she said to Jack.

"Are you sure?" he said. "We don't know when it's supposed to go off."

"No—no thyme! The herb! It's not here!"

"No call for it," said the chef.

"But, I thought for sure..." said Penny.

Suddenly, there was a meow from under the counter. Then another one, loud and insistent. "Dinglebat!" said Penny, crouching to look underneath the stainless surface.

There was Dinglebat, covered in flour, on a little shelf next to an empty container labeled "yeast."

"Dinglebat!"

"MEOW!" he said, and if cats could yell, it would definitely have been a yell.

Jack crouched down and opened the canister. Inside was a blinking blue light. And that light was attached to a smaller metal canister.

"They saved the yeast, Penny, and left it here."

"You found it!" said Penny.

"*We* found it," said Jack.

"MEOW!" said Dinglebat.

"Okay, right—technically you found it," Jack said, "but *we* free-associated ideas until it got us here. If we hadn't gotten here to the kitchen, you wouldn't have found it, so there you go. You shouldn't claim all the glory."

The cat looked down sadly.

"Well, you mostly did it yourself," said Jack, trying to cheer it up.

The cat nodded, then starting licking flour off its paws.

"What is that thing with the lights?" said the cook.

"It's a thing that shouldn't be here in the kitchen," said Penny.

"It's yours?"

"No, it's not, but we're taking it."

"You know, it's not yours. And you're not supposed to be in here, honestly, and a cat most definitely isn't supposed to be in here."

"And he WAS going to karate chop my neck!" added the waitress.

"Wait—you heard me say that?" said Penny.

"I couldn't do it," said Jack as he carefully lifted the device out of the canister. Penny scooped up Dinglebat.

"Just wait a minute," said the cook, flipping patties as he did so, "I think we need to call security before anything else..."

Jack knocked an open bottle of vegetable oil onto the stovetop before the chef could finish his sentence. Some spilled into the burner beneath and ignited the entire surface, expensive meat and all. The chef, yelling and cursing, grabbed for the fire extinguisher.

"RUN!" yelled Jack.

And they did, Jack cradling the bomb and Penny cradling Dinglebat. The waitress tried to trip Penny as they went through the door and out into an adjoining dining area. A few people looked up, then went back to their smart phones and dinners. Suddenly, the sound of an alarm shrieked through the hotel.

"Yep, we caught the kitchen on fire," said Jack.

They were now on their way outside via the pool area. Beyond the pool was a large artificial lake, lit by the evening sun. Jack wondered how many gallons needed to be added to the lake per day to keep up with evaporation loss. *Maybe it's spring-fed?* They ran past the pool and back around to where a few dumpsters were cleverly concealed by pink brick walls.

"It's crazy that something so small could blow up a whole hotel!" said Penny, panting at Jack. "What do we do with it now?" Jack considered chucking it in a dumpster, then realized that if it could blow up an entire building, it would make short work of a dumpster.

Behind them, the hotel was now in full panic mode. People streamed out all of the doors and alarms screamed. Someone was making an announcement about "leaving in an orderly manner," but it wasn't looking very orderly thus far. Smoke was pouring out of one side of the building. Meanwhile, from the other doors people were shuffling out, thinking the fire alarm must be a drill.

Then came the voice again over the intercom. "This is not a drill!" Now people started speeding up. One fat man fell into the pool.

Jack had to get rid of this bomb—but how?

"How should I get rid of it?" he yelled in frustration.

THROW IT IN THE LAKE!

"Are you sure I should throw it in the lake?" Jack replied.

"What?" Penny answered. "I didn't say to throw it in the lake."

YES, THROW IT IN THE LAKE!

"The lake it is," said Jack.

"Are you sure we should throw it into the lake?" asked Penny. "What if it blows up the lake?"

"Who cares if it blows up the lake!?" said Jack. "If it blows up the lake, we'll all get wet, so what?"

"What about the ducks?" Penny pointed to a mother duck followed by seven adorable baby ducks.

"Oh, come on," Jack said. "Would you rather I hold on to it?"

"And the puppy!?"

On one side of a lake, an incredibly cute white puppy was watching the ducks.

"Look, I mean, a puppy is..."

"And what about the beautiful koi?"

"Beautiful what?"

"How about I hold it?" A meaty fist snatched the blinking blue object from Jack's hand.

It was security!

"Stay right there," said a second voice. More security.

Jack looked. They didn't have guns. And they looked slower than him.

"Arsonists, I assume?" said the first voice.

"No, not us!" said Penny.

"Then why are you hiding behind the dumpsters with flour on your blouse?"

"Flour?" Penny looked down. It was true. "But," she said, wheeling, "what does flour have to do with arson?"

"An arson in the kitchen might have a lot to do with flour!" said the guard, unperturbed.

Behind them, people were yelling and arguing in the parking lot. Some were screaming about items left behind, others were searching for family and friends. Jack heard sirens approaching.

"What is this thing here?" asked the guard with the bomb.

Jack decided that answering "It's a bomb" would be a bad idea, so he might as well keep up the streak of lies.

"It's a bass cannon."

"A bass cannon?" the man said, "Well, isn't that interesting. And do you use these bass cannons for lighting fires, then?"

"That's ridiculous," Jack said. "They're not loud enough for that. Though maybe you could get close with a totally pumping amp. Or if you played a really hot single. But even then..."

He had to get that bomb. If it went off now, his career as an international gardening mystery super spy agent of renown would end. He didn't want to be the guy who died in the first movie. He'd seen that before. Penny was looking back and forth between Jack and the bomb, nervously biting her lip.

"Maybe your girlfriend here could tell us how to use a bass cannon to light fires, then?" the second security guy said. "Maybe she's the one with the, how did you call it, 'totally pumping amp'?"

Penny shook her head. "No, we're innocent. Just give us our bass cannon back. We need to go find our friends and make sure they're okay."

EVERYTHING IS A WEAPON.

"Yeah, I don't think so," said the security guy holding the bomb. "I think we'll all just stay right here for a little bit. You, me, your boyfriend, and the bass cannon. Let's see what the police have to say about— AHHHHHHH!!!"

The man screamed and so did Penny. She screamed because she was startled by his scream, but his scream was because a coconut shell shirt button had just gone through his left arm. The other guard rushed Jack, only knowing that he had seen the young man had thrown something that had hurt his co-worker.

Jack ripped another button off his shirt but before he could throw it, the second guard was on top of him. Penny took the distraction to snag the bomb from the wounded security guard, who seemed to have lost all the fight in him.

The guard was bigger and much heavier, but Jack escaped his hold, then grabbed a handful of reeds and slashed it across the man's back so hard it tore open his shirt and raised bleeding welts. With a scream of pain, the man raced at him in a blind fury, but Jack side-stepped and allowed the guard's momentum to carry him farther. He then executed a move known as the "sipa sa ilalim," hitting the man with a flying kick to the posterior that send him face-first into the muddy shoreline.

Penny looked at him, impressed, but there was no time to bask in her approval. Jack held out his hand, and she handed him the bomb. "I'm throwing it in the lake, Penny—get down!" Jack ordered. She ducked down inside the dumpster enclosure without a word.

With a run towards the water and a mighty heave, Jack threw the canister end-over-end, over the heads of eight puzzled ducks and a glinting collection of lazily drifting koi, almost to the middle of the lake where a fountain was busily contributing to the draining of an already threatened underground aquifer. The adorable puppy watched avidly as the canister twirled through the air in a high arc.

It hit the water—and then a mighty concussion boomed—FROM BEHIND THEM! Jack had only a moment to wonder why the lake's surface was so still despite all the noise before he found himself thrown over the ducks and koi.

CHAPTER FOURTEEN

"You drank half the lake before Penny fished you out."

Jack's eyes tried to focus. He thought a vat of margarine was hanging above his face, but the Country Crock slowly congealed into Pak's unreadable features.

"What?" Jack mumbled.

"You're alive. You found the bomb. Sort of. Well, you blew it up."

"I..."

"Yes," said Pak. "You threw the detonator into the lake."

"The glowy thing was the detonator? That means I..."

"Blew up the hotel, yes. But most everyone was out. Except for stubborn people who ignore fire drills. And Koreans tied to chairs."

"Oh," said Jack. "Guess I'm going to jail, then."

Pak shook his head, then winced. He had bandages on it.

"I keep forgetting I should not shake my head yes or no."

"Yeah, tell me about it," Jack said. "Why all the bandages?"

"They had to drill into my head."

"Yowch."

"Only a little," said Pak. "I should be fine again soon. Can't do much for now, though."

"So... why am I not going to jail again?" Jack asked. "Because I must have killed a few people."

"Yes, but we will take care of that. Part of our benefits program. You did very well. So did she," he said, gesturing at someone Jack couldn't see.

The person walked closer—it was Penny.

"Hi Penny," said Jack, suddenly wondering how long he'd been in this hospital bed.

"Hi Jack. Glad you're back," Penny said, patting him on the arm.

Jack grinned. "Is this the part where you lean down and give the brave hero a kiss?"

"No," she said.

Jack shrugged.

"Loser!" rasped a voice from the other side of the curtain.

"Who's a loser?" said Jack.

"Your mom!"

Jack frowned. Apparently the man next door was well enough to be a jerk. *But perhaps the guy is dying, or in a bad way, and the emotions are getting to him. Be compassionate, Jack.*

"Listen, friend, I hope you get better," Jack said, realizing that his own voice was almost as raspy.

"Eat paint and die," replied the man.

"Okay," said Jack, "I'm doing that right now," he said in a cheerful voice.

He winked at Penny and Pak, then made slurping sounds.

"Are you dead yet?" rasped the man.

"Quite dead," Jack replied. "As a doorknob."

The man remained silent. *Well, nice to have cleared that up.*

"It was a very nice hotel before you blew it up," said Pak.

"Yeah," said Jack.

"My iPad, purse and clothes were back up in my room," said Penny. "You owe me."

"Oh, come on," said Jack.

"I've already inventoried their value, along with the cost of finding new reservations," said Penny. "So you can just write a check. I had a nice pair of 501s."

"What?"

"Jeans. Nice jeans."

"Ah," said Jack, "I was hoping they were some sort of new-fangled potato cannon."

"Jack?" said Pak. "We've got more info."

"Go for it, Pak," Jack said.

"They were using a fungal toxin on their victims," Pak said. "One of our people identified it in your bloodstream."

"Like magic mushrooms?" Jack asked.

Pak nodded.

"$1,213.67," said Penny.

"Meow," said Dinglebat.

Dinglebat? thought Jack. He was pretty sure cats were not allowed into hospitals. Except maybe for stupid hospitals in an areas with lots of rich old people. But this was a normal person hospital, as the cheap 80s-era drop ceiling attested. He wondered if this was the one that gave you hepatitis, or the one that performed stitches with cheap fishing line.

"You're crazy," he told Penny. "I'm not paying you anything."

"You can pay me with a kiss," she said.

"That would be overpaying," said Jack.

"I was just kidding anyway," she sniffed.

Jack rolled his eyes and turned to Pak. "Tell me about the Koreans—what are they really doing?"

"Pretty simple, Jack. They drug people with their psychedelic mushroom drug, then pry for information about other soil scientists and organizations which practice agriculture related to poisons, chemical fertilizers, turning the soil, et cetera. Then they release the drugged victim into a very harsh natural area for the ecosystem to dispose of."

"How do you know this?"

"Google."

"Google?"

"No, just kidding. It is what we have pieced together. Our agents have been working on it for weeks now."

"But they're still out there, Pak. The rest of them?"

Pak frowned. "Yes. We believe they are regrouping now. They know we are onto them. This would be the time to press forward and take them out—yet we have very few available agents. The world is a dangerous place, and we are few, and our leader is gone. And I," he tapped his bandaged head, "am not going anywhere for a while."

"Snickers," Jack said.

"Excuse me?" said Pak.

"Snickers. The nurse. Oh shoot—is this the hospital where I threw the coke at the nurse?"

"I missed this story," said Pak.

"Yeah, you were unconscious. Allenette was the nurse when I brought you in. I was trying to buy her a Diet Coke, but I ended up throwing it at her after beating down a cop with his uniform pants."

Pak blinked.

"It wasn't my finest hour."

"Jack," Pak said, "I don't believe we can do anything about the Koreans for now. You are beat up, and I am as well."

"You're right, Pak, but look what they did to Hardin. Look what they did to the hotel. The only way to keep weeds from becoming an infestation is to decapitate them early, preferably with a hula hoe."

"There is some truth to that," Pak said, "but what can we do?"

"We go for them, right now."

"No, Jack, we can't," Pak said. "We need to sit this round out."

Jack threw his hands up with a clatter of tubes. "You sit it out, Pak— I'm going after them."

"You are beat up, too," said Pak. "I will talk to my superiors. You realize this is crazy, right?"

"Sometimes it is the crazy ideas that work, Pak," Penny chimed in.

"She's right," Jack said. "And I owe Hardin. And... I have some sort of extra help, from... who knows what. Look how much we've gotten done so far—despite me knowing nothing. Pak, I saved you from being tied up, I killed a guy who was going to kill me-"

He was interrupted by the rasping voice of the patient in the next bed "I wish he had—you're supposed to be dead!"

Jack ignored him, "I found a bomb—sort of—and I got Pak to the hospital when he needed help, plus I got away from the cops, and I-"

Jack was going to say, "fought a pair of meathead security guards," but a terrifying figure walked in.

The nurse. That nurse.

She walked over, eyebrow arched, one hand on her hip. In her other hand she held a folder filled with papers.

"Hey, weirdo," she said to Jack, tapping him on the chest. "I brought you some light entertainment. Just hide them under your pillow when you're done looking—they're sort of, uh, private."

She tossed the thick folder onto his lap and winked at him, took a look at his chart, then walked out.

Penny raised her eyebrows. "Sort of private? Is there something you're hiding from us?"

Jack picked up the folder and opened it. X-rays. Horrible, horrible x-rays. He showed the first one to Penny, who looked close for a second, then recoiled in horror.

Pak leaned over for a look and winced. "Perhaps you should stay here with your friend and enjoy the pictures, then later fight against forces of evil?"

"No, I'm settled. That's the easy way out, Pak," said Jack, "which means it's the wrong way out. I don't think I'm injured that badly."

Penny nodded. "They said you should be out in a few days."

"I'm going to shoot for one day," Jack said.

"That would be good, Jack," Pak said. "Time is short. But still I think you should not go. It would be a suicide mission."

"Pak is right," Penny said. "If you go in there, Jack, what are you going to do? You can't fight them all. Unless you just find them and call the police.'

"Right, Penny," Pak said. "I do not see much you can do, Jack, other than get killed. We have not pinned anything to these men that the police can use. We are a clandestine organization—if we went right to the police on this, there would be an investigation. Names would come out. And operations. We get away with many things due to special diplomatic status, yet we must be jacket and knife sometimes."

Jack shrugged and settled back. He idly picked up a second x-ray and immediately wished he hadn't. Then Pak's phone rang. He answered in Mandarin, then his eyes widened in shock. He listened for a short while, speaking rarely, then hung up and exhaled heavily.

"What is it, Pak?" said Penny. "You look like you've seen a ghost."

"Master Rice," he said quietly so the other patient wouldn't hear. "They have him—and he's alive. For the moment."

"For the moment?" Jack said.

Pak nodded, then immediately stopped and winced yet again.

"One of our men spied out their compound from the air and got a glimpse of him. He does not appear to be under heavy guard, either."

"So what—a few agents can go in and get him?"

"No," Pak said. "Looks like it must be you. You can go in and get him."

"Me? I thought you just said I couldn't do it?"

"I agree—my superiors do not. They wish for you to go in."

"That decides it then," said Jack.

"Wait," said Penny, "you're really going to do it?"

Jack raised an eyebrow at her. "Yes."

Pak looked worried. "I don't know why they want you to go. This makes little sense to me, as you know little of our ways, are not a trained agent, and will not even be able to speak the language! And you'll be alone."

"No," Penny said. "He won't be. I'll go too."

They both turned to look at Penny. Her face was grimly determined.

"It will be very dangerous, Penny," Pak said.

"I know what I'm doing," she replied. "I know it's dangerous. But I have help."

On cue, Dinglebat stuck his head out of her purse.

Pak sighed. "You cannot bring your cat on the plane."

"He's a service animal," she said.

"Meow?" Dinglebat said.

"No dominoes," Pak said. "You have to leave him with me. Cats are not safe in Korea.

Dinglebat jumped gracefully onto Pak's shoulder, making him wince.

"Careful, animal—I am not in peak form," Pak said, carefully setting the kitten onto a chair. "I recommend you hide in case the nurse returns." Dinglebat did so, much to Pak's surprise.

"Smart cat," he said.

Penny nodded. "Probably smarter than Jack and me."

"That is quite possible," Pak agreed.

✳ ✳ ✳

Sometime in the very early morning, Jack awakened. The room was silent, except for the occasional *bloop* of a medical monitor. He really needed something but couldn't figure out what it was. *Water?* He looked at the IV drip in his arm. *No, I'm hydrated. Maybe I need to use the restroom?* Then he looked down with a wince at another tube emerging from the sheets. *Nope.*

Then it hit him. It had been at least twenty-four hours since his last *Ocean Octave!* That had to be some kind of record. He wondered if he should hit the red button with the picture of a nurse on it. *She would almost certainly get me some, especially if I talk lightly about scabs first.*

Or maybe, just maybe, I'll be able to go without them this time? Jack admitted to himself that *Ocean Octaves!* didn't make him feel all that great. He always wanted them, but after pigging out on a bag, he didn't become a better person, or gain muscle mass. The seaweed was likely high in micronutrients, but the preservatives couldn't be doing any good. And it contained soy. If there is one thing a mysterious international agricultural spy of repute shouldn't do, it is to eat testosterone-damping products.

Maybe Penny would get him some. Maybe he could call her? If she was willing to go on a suicide mission with him, surely she'd go on a store run! There had to be a 24-hour place that sold *Ocean Octaves!* No. He could live without the *Ocean Octaves!* He knew it. He would go back to sleep...

Wait, what am I doing?

While talking to himself, Jack had disconnected the IV and the catheter and now found his feet on the floor. *There's no way you're going to find any in this hospital, Jack! Give it up.*

You're right, he thought as he walked unsteadily to the window, pushed aside the curtain and looked out. He was on the second floor.

It is entirely too dangerous and ridiculous to climb out of a second-storey window, in your condition, to get a snack food you already know isn't good for you, he thought as he climbed out the window and onto a small ledge. He wasn't all that high from the ground, but it would be a rough drop. Maybe he could grab the sheet and do the old rope trick?

Then he heard something in the room behind him. He ducked, hanging onto the edge of the window. A very disconcerting breeze wafted through the back of his hospital gown, and he hoped no one was looking up from below.

The door was open. *That nurse?* he thought, but to his horror, he saw an Asian man in dark scrubs creeping into the room.

Jack hunched at the sill, hoping the slight movement of the curtains in the breeze wouldn't draw the man's attention. They didn't. The man looked at Jack's empty bed, then went to the other side of the divider.

What if that guy is here to kill me—he must be here to kill me—and he thinks the other patient is me in the dim light and kills him? That would be terrible! Jack scrambled through the window back into the room. Adrenaline coursed into his bloodstream. He looked around for something he could use in a fight.

JACK—USE YOUR GOWN!

"No," Jack whispered. "I am not taking my clothes off!"

"Who are you!?" called a raspy voice.

Jack almost answered before he realized it was the other patient talking to the intruder. Then there was the sound of choking—he had to save the man! He grabbed the metal lamp from his bedside, popped the plug out of the wall, and threw aside the curtain between the beds.

He hoped no one was looking up from below.

The Korean stopped throttling the old man and yanked his hands up as Jack swung the lamp. He easily parried the blow and grabbed at the lamp in an attempt to wrest it from Jack's admittedly weak grasp.

I TOLD YOU TO USE YOUR ROBE!

"How is that better than a metal lamp, nutjob?" Jack gasped as the Korean jerked the lamp away and Jack fell backwards onto his bed.

JUST DO IT!

Jack said a few bad things, yanked off his robe, and wadded it up into a ball.

The Korean stepped toward him with the lamp.

"Get back!" Jack said, brandishing the ball of thin, flower-printed cotton.

The Korean shook his head and took another step—just in time to get hit with the gown. It barely glanced off his shoulder, but the blow spun the man around and threw him hard into a huge beige monitor by his almost-victim's bed, killing him instantly.

"Whoa," Jack said, feeling for a pulse and finding nothing. "That was unexpected."

The old man in the other bed grabbed his pillow and began hitting the dead Korean with it.

"Sir, I think he's dead. I think we should probably throw him out the window."

"I like the way you think," choked out the man, with a wheezing laugh.

Jack dragged the body across the floor towards the window, finding it quite difficult. He was about halfway there when the door opened. Jack turned, horrified to see that another dark figure was entering the room.

"Need help?" it whispered.

The guy looked Korean. But he was offering to help?

"Agent 10-10-10," the man said. "At your service."

Jack sighed in relief. Then Jack realized he was naked.

"You have the situation under control?" the agent said, pointing to the dead Korean.

"Oh yes, mostly."

"Mostly?"

"Yes," said Jack. "We just need to throw him out the window."

The agent raised an eyebrow.

"What, is that not okay?" Jack asked. "I mean, seriously. Aren't we supposed to be cold-blooded super-secret sleuths of international mystery?"

"We are gardeners first, Jack."

"So!?"

"So we cannot compost him if he is splattered on the sidewalk and picked up by the authorities."

"Good point," said Jack. Compost your enemies, he thought. Someone should print that on a T-shirt.

* * *

Jack dreamed that there was a bug on his forehead. Then he decided there really was a bug on his forehead. He snapped awake to find that nurse picking at his face with her nail.

"Hey!" he yelped.

"Sorry," she said. "Scab."

Jack made a disgusted face, and she shrugged.

"What did you do to this place?" she asked. "And why are you all disconnected?"

"What do you mean?" said Jack, playing innocent. He suddenly realized he was under the sheet, but missing his gown. He glanced around the room but didn't see it. Probably it was on the other side of the divider. With the lamp. The dead man was gone.

"The patient in the other bed. His side was a mess. He said you did it, though he also claimed a guy broke in and tried to choke him and that you fought him off."

"People like to dream about me," Jack said.

"Oh yeah? He said you wanted to throw a Viet Cong soldier out the window."

"Sounds like a great dream. Like I said, people can't help these sorts of dreams about me. I'm very interesting."

"Well, Mr. Interesting, you need to get hooked back up, at least to the IV. And you need a gown."

Jack winced. He had hoped she wouldn't notice.

She tossed a new gown onto his bed.

"Need help putting it on?" she said, taking a swig from her Diet Coke.

"No," said Jack.

"I'm not leaving until you put it on," she said.

"Okay, fine," said Jack. "But do I at least get a little privacy?"

"Sure, no problem. I'm a professional," she said, looking away as Jack threw his legs over the side of the bed. As he dressed, she rooted under his pillow for the x-rays. "I always take care of my patients' privacy. Nice traps, by the way."

There was a knock at the door, then it swung open as Jack struggled to tie up the back of his gown.

It was Penny, and her eyes widened as she took in the scene: a half-clothed Jack, and a nurse sitting on his bed with an x-ray collection.

"Am I interrupting something?" she asked.

The nurse smirked at her. "Just making sure my favorite patient gets dressed. Now lay back down and give me your arm," she said to Jack. He complied, and she reattached the IV. "You want the catheter too?" she asked.

"No," said Jack. "You have done enough. You can leave me alone now."

The nurse patted his shoulder and got up to leave. "I'll do that."

She was almost out of the room when Jack spoke. "Wait," he said. "When can I get out of here?"

The nurse shrugged. "Not my call. You'll have to talk to the doc."

"And the doc—when will he be around?"

"Later today, I'm sure," said the nurse. "If you get bored, just ring me." And she was gone.

Penny sniffed, then turned to Jack, who was now standing by the bed, as fully clothed as a man can be in a hospital gown.

"Jack, Pak says there was trouble last night?"

"Yeah, trouble. A Korean came here, probably to kill me. But he tried to choke the wrong guy."

"He tried to choke you?"

"No, I wasn't speaking figuratively. I meant literally. He tried to choke the guy in the next bed, but he meant to choke me instead, but got mixed up in the dark. Probably they only gave him my room number."

"Wow," said Penny. "How did he miss you? You were in the first bed?"

Jack considered telling her the about his abortive *Ocean Octaves!* run, but decided that wouldn't paint him in a particularly good light.

"Well, I dodged him."

"Dodged him?"

"Yep. Then I tried to hit him with my lamp when he started choking the old guy."

"And you knocked him out?"

"No, not exactly," said Jack. "I couldn't hurt him with the lamp, so I ripped off my gown."

She looked at him as if had spit a wombat on the linoleum.

Jack shrugged. "I didn't want to do it. It was just that was what the voice in my head said to do. He told me to use the gown as a weapon."

She moved back as if the orally ejected wombat was foaming at the mouth and sitting on Jack's shoulder.

"Oh, come on, Penny. You have a 'bomb-sniffing cat'. Are you seriously going to get weird because I have a voice in my head?"

"Dinglebat is one, though."

"And I have one," said Jack. "A voice in my head, that is."

"And your voice in your head tells you to take off your clothes?"

"No, of course not," said Jack. "I mean, not normally. Just this time. It said, 'Everything is a weapon,' but when I tried to use the lamp as a weapon it changed its mind." Jack stopped and thought about it for a second. "Come to think of it, that doesn't really make much sense."

"That's what I'm saying," said Penny.

"No, it's not the voice that doesn't make sense. That's strange, of course, but it's not unheard of. The Old Testament saints heard from God, right?"

"Sure," said Penny, "I guess so. But did God tell them to take their clothes off?"

"He told Moses to take off his sandals," Jack exclaimed.

"Right," said Penny, "and then to use them as throwing stars, I suppose?"

"No, no, well, this isn't God. I don't think. Not *the* God."

Penny sighed. "Jack, I think you've been hit on the head too many times."

Jack shrugged. "Maybe. I don't know. I do know that I get this strange ability to make ordinary things into weapons when I'm under stress or forced into a corner."

"But not lamps?"

"Apparently not," said Jack. "Apparently the gown was better."

"The gown? You killed him with a cotton gown? How?"

"I'm not sure. Maybe it was the touch—the feel?"

"The fabric that ends your life?" Penny threw her hands up. "No, that doesn't make any sense, Jack. I mean, the gown is made of soft material. The lamp was metal, right?"

"Right," said Jack. "Hard stuff. Like the leg of the love seat. It should have worked."

"The leg of a love seat?"

"Yep," said Jack. "That was before you. I threw a love seat leg through a guy's chest."

"Great," said Penny. "You said something about that earlier, but it didn't sink in."

"No, of course it didn't. It went right through," Jack said, exasperated.

"I think I'm going to go now," Penny said. "You need rest."

"No, Penny—don't go. I can do it again."

"I'd rather you didn't throw a love seat leg through my chest."

"No, not you," Jack said. "I like you. This was a bad guy."

"So you want to find another bad guy and throw a love seat leg through his chest to demonstrate to me that you're not crazy and that I should stick around?"

"Sure, why not?" said Jack.

"I am going to blame this on your head injuries," said Penny.

"Oh, come on," said Jack. "Here, let me just take off the pillowcase." He did, wadding it up into a ball.

"I should be able to throw this thing so hard it puts a serious mark on that wall," he said, pointing to the pastel-pink plaster across the room. She crossed her arms across her chest, unconvinced. "Watch," said Jack, winding back and throwing the fabric as hard as he could.

The pillowcase arced across the room and hit the wall harmlessly, falling to the glossy floor. The wall showed no sign of damage.

"I don't get it," said Jack. "I threw a button into a guy's arm the other day at the dumpsters. Didn't you see that?"

"I wasn't sure what you did," said Penny. "I figured you nailed him with something dangerous. Like a little throwing knife or something."

"Nope," said Jack. "It was a button. Made of coconut shell."

"I'm just not going for this, Jack," said Penny.

Jack paced over and picked up the pillowcase.

"Come on, Steroid Voice—where are you?" Jack mumbled, but he heard nothing in return.

He wound up and threw the pillowcase as hard as he could, with no more success than on the first try.

Penny looked at him.

"Look, Penny," he started.

"No, it's not a big deal," she said. "You've been through a lot. And you were attacked last night, and fought the guy off. That's great. We'll wait for you to get better, then we'll go save Master Rice, and then you can demonstrate your mad skills."

"Fine," Jack said. "Just you wait."

CHAPTER FIFTEEN

"This flight is going to last forever," Penny complained as she fidgeted in her seat. "Why is Korea so far?"

"Actually," Jack said, "it's only a few more hours before the layover in Dubai, then a few more hours on a plane before until London, then a few more hours before the layover in Miami, then–"

"Wait a minute—I think you're reading that backwards," Penny said, snatching the itinerary from Jack's hand.

"Oh," she said after a minute, "that is weird."

"We'll make it there eventually," Jack assured her. "I think we should take this time to plan our attack and then, maybe, share the parts of our personal back-stories with each other that will interest the readers in our lives. So—do you like gardening?"

"Gardening?" Penny said. "Like azaleas and stuff?"

"No," said Jack. "Azaleas are the most boring plant in the world, except for the five minutes they look amazing in spring. Edibles, Penny. You know, like turnips. Turnips are exciting."

"I don't think I've ever eaten a turnip. And I live in an apartment."

"But you have a balcony, right? Don't you have a plant on your balcony or something?"

"Oh yes," Penny said. "I forgot all about it. I have one of those ones with the leaves."

"With the leaves?"

"The white and green leaves. It was a present from somebody."

"*Dracaena?*"

"No, not a vampire."

"No," Jack said, irritated. "Was it a *Dracaena*? A *Dracaena* is a type of plant."

"I don't think so," Penny said.

"But it is variegated?"

"No, it's just one type."

"Dang it, Penny." Jack slapped his knee in exasperation. "You really don't know anything about plants, do you?"

She looked at him petulantly, wrinkling her nose. "So?"

Jack shook his head in disgust. He'd thought more of this girl. First his pastor, now Penny. The world was a messed up place, full of ignorance and folly.

"I had a Chia Pet once," Penny volunteered, hoping to cheer him up.

"And it died?" said Jack, viciously.

Penny winced. "Well, yeah. But it grew for a while."

Jack shook his head. "Never mind gardening. Let's talk about the target."

Penny nodded and reached into her purse, looking around to make sure they weren't observed, then pulled out a folder with photos in it.

"Here's the place we need to go," she said, handing the folder to Jack.

He glanced through the photos. "Interesting—mostly pines here. A woodland. And these guys by the cabin, they're our target."

"Yep," Penny said. "While you were out, my agency and your people had a chat and gave me these."

"What's inside the dome?" Jack asked, pointing to a structure in the trees.

"We don't know," Penny said.

"And Penny, tell me—why did they suddenly decide to send you and me? I was going to go on my own to avenge Hardin, yet Pak didn't like that idea, then suddenly—you know, this isn't making any sense to me, in retrospect. We are babes in the woods. Well, you're a babe in the woods. Not that you'd be able to ID any trees. I'm more of a hunk by a trunk, actually, but–"

"I don't know, Jack," Penny said, taking his hand. "But I'm glad I'm going with you."

Jack felt ambivalent. Non-gardeners had that effect on him. He didn't return the squeeze of her hand and after a moment, she let go.

"Is it a dumb cane?" Jack ventured.

"A what?" Penny said.

"*Dieffenbachia*," he said. "Your plant."

"I have no idea," she said. "I haven't even looked at it in a long time."

Jack knew it. It was probably wilting right now—or dead. *Why did people have to be this way?* He shook it off. "Forget about it, let's concentrate on business."

"Okay," Penny said.

"So tell me—this place here, this bit of woods, it's private land? In South Korea, right?"

"Right on the second, not on the first. It's a nationally protected woodland. Remote. They must have built the dome and everything in bits and pieces. There are logging roads."

"And we just stroll in, two white people—unarmed—and rescue Master Rice?"

"That's the plan," said Penny. "Pak suggested we dress like tourists and play clueless."

"That will be easy," Jack said. "I've never even been out of the US before. But our clothes aren't exactly hiking clothes."

"We'll get some at a shop," Penny said. "Shopping is fun."

Jack made a face.

"Oh, come on—I'll help you find some really nice stuff."

"Great. Sounds like fun."

"Yep," Penny said.

Jack disappeared into his thoughts as Penny studied a map.

So she doesn't like plants. Or worse, she doesn't care about plants. Yet we're together in this thing. Even if she's an untrustworthy person, we have to have each other's backs. Jack remembered seeing her in her swimsuit. *And she has a nice back. A really nice back. Rounded shoulders, delicate neck. A perfectly curving spinal column. Very feminine vertebrae and nice, smooth skin with...*

"What are you thinking?" Penny asked.

"Palmer Method?" Jack sputtered.

"Is that golf?"

"No," he said. "No, I was thinking we're together in this thing. And I really know almost nothing about you."

She laughed. "Ah, so that was the faraway look."

Jack nodded. "Yes, exactly. That was it."

"Well," Penny said, "I was an army brat."

"Yeah?"

"Yeah. We moved all over the place. Dad was a mechanic, worked at a string of bases, mostly in the US. We were at Ft. Benning a while."

"That's a tough place to grow up. Hard ground, bad rainfall. Acid mix of clay and sand."

"Uh, yeah, I guess. The housing was bad too. We were also in Alaska. Ft. Greely."

"Yikes," said Jack. "That's gotta be, what? USDA Zone 3?"

"What are you talking about?" Penny said.

"You know, the hardiness zone map."

Penny looked at him blankly.

"Never mind," said Jack. "It's no wonder you never got into gardening. You kept moving, and you were in lousy conditions."

"Right..." Penny said, sarcastically. "I think you really have a one-track mind. I suppose you don't want to hear about the puppy I lost to rabid caribou? Or the time my favorite dress got covered in used motor oil? Or how I got roped into my current black-ops job?"

"I'm interested in all of the above, Penny," Jack said, trying to be conciliatory.

"None of them involve gardening, Jack."

"That's true," Jack said. *Therefore they really aren't all that interesting.* "But," he thought for a moment, diving deep into his knowledge of the female of the species, "I'm interested in you, too."

"More than my Dracula plant?"

"More than your what?"

She rolled her eyes. "You're hopeless. But I'll tell you how I got roped in. See, when I was a teenager I was wandering around the base and came upon a mysterious building. It was locked up, yet I figured out how to..."

Jack tuned her out. *I wonder what kind of corn varieties they grow in Korea? It's a temperate climate—maybe flint? Or would they be all GMO? Or perhaps they concentrated on rice and haven't done much at all with Zea mays? I'll bet Customs would take any seeds I got, though.*

He continued thinking along these lines for about a half-hour, nodding occasionally to Penny as she talked.

"...and when the temporal disturbance ended, he was more than a kitten..."

Maybe squash species. Some of them ought to thrive in Virginia. I could nab a few fruit from a local market. Those were often great places to track down interesting vegetables. But do they have markets in Korea like that? Probably. Farmer's Markets in the US were good, so why not...

"...and I had to come through the portal in my underwear because of the force field..."

And if I could get some pumpkin seeds and hide them, I could probably also hit a garden supply store. Get some really different things. Maybe they had Korean turnips that would work back home? And turnips, perhaps—or was that just the Japanese...

"...total black ops, I'm sure of it now, but maybe not our guys..."

Actually, maybe I don't want their vegetables if they taste like the food I ate. But that could just be the fermentation or the spices. Or even the drug. Some fungi are quite bitter. If that were the case, perhaps we could warn people about bitter foods—but no, that would be impossible. Too many people could be targets and they'd just switch tactics once the word got out that we were on to them...

"...and I appeared next to a big tree, right there in the—"

Jack snapped back into the moment. "What kind of a tree?"

"I don't know," Penny said. "It was a big one, though."

"Broad leaves? Narrow? Lanceolate?"

"What?" Penny said. "That's all you care about? Not the fact that I was ripped through time?"

"You were?" said Jack.

Penny stared at him blackly, reached into her purse, pulled out an e-reader, and didn't speak again until they went through three layovers and landed at long last in Korea.

CHAPTER SIXTEEN

It's a good thing a lot of Koreans speak English, Jack thought for the thirtieth time. He handed Penny a hot dog and thanked the vendor, then he and Penny rode their scooters out of the city and into the countryside.

He had been amazed by the sheer quantity of people in Korea. And the sheer quantity of scooters and bicycles. The city was dense and loud, exciting, with strange and exotic smells and music. But now they were leaving it behind, headed towards a showdown.

Penny was speaking to him again, albeit in a perfunctory manner. She'd gotten them both clothing and managed to book a pair of hotel rooms. The clothing store seemed to be a tasteless L. L. Bean knockoff joint, and Jack was now dressed like someone from a catalog. Provided the catalog was put out by a colorblind redneck. Orange hiking boots, grey synthetic material pants that were supposed to dry instantly, woolen socks, a green ski cap, and a red plaid jacket.

When he'd asked Penny about the need for woolen socks, she'd looked at him like he had three eyes. "Of course you need wool socks! Didn't you know that? They're much better for your feet."

"Why," Jack said, "do sheep do a lot of hiking?"

Penny threw the socks at him.

Jack was conflicted about Penny. He liked her, but she didn't like plants. And he liked plants, so he shouldn't like her. People who liked plants were trustworthy, people who didn't were suspect. It was that simple. *Quit worrying about it, Jack. There are plenty of other fish in the sea.*

Somehow Jack hadn't pictured himself on a scooter when he imagined life as a multi-national gardening agent of incomprehensible background and intentions. His scooter was silver and purple and had a weird cartoon mouse on the side which appeared to be licking its left ear. Not cool, but he decided to own it, as if he always fought international criminals while riding something that looked like it was designed for a high school anime fangirl.

"It's a place called Keun Beoseos Park, Jack!" Penny shouted at him.

"Coon Bus Ales Park—sounds like a craft brewer."

"No. It's Keun Beoseos Park. It means 'big mushroom' park."

"Nice. I like mushrooms. How long until we get to their camp?"

"Probably only forty minutes or so."

They rode along, the air cool. There were a few deciduous trees beside the road, though many of the trees were pines. Jack wished he could stop and walk through the woods, but remembered Hardin. Hardin required blood. *I wonder if he's still in the dugout.*

There is probably a better way I could have handled that, Jack thought, but waved it off. Hardin had liked baseball.

There were more important things to worry about now. Like the voice in his head. What was it? Was it just him? A buried splinter of himself? Yet it really sounded like a voice in his ear. He knew if he shared the experience with a doctor they'd pump him up with antipsychotic drugs or something. Though much of the day he'd been drugged was now a blur, he remembered quite well the terrible ice cream flavors and the conversation he'd had with the strange figure in brown.

Strange, though, that the power he possessed only really worked in a fight. He'd tried throwing paper cups, pens, napkins, tongue depressors and other objects in the hospital. Nothing had happened. Even in his hotel room last night he'd paced around, trying to think fighting thoughts, while chucking wadded pieces of note paper at imaginary assailants. They flew about the room in a normal fashion, refusing to leave even slight impact craters on the room walls.

Yet he had thrown that love seat leg through a man's chest. And put big slashes on a guard's back with a fistful of pond reeds. And beat a cop with his own pants. And killed a man with a wadded-up robe.

But how? How? It made little sense, but there must be some logic to it. The only time he'd been able to converse with the thing in his head had been in the midst of a fight or when he was drugged. The idea of taking drugs and entering a dream state where he could talk with Mr. Steroid Voice struck him as a bad idea. But starting a fight as a conversation piece was also nuts.

He just had to hope that part of his personality—or that entity, which assured him it wasn't a demon—would appear when he needed him.

"Here!" said Penny, pointing to a wooden sign in Korean beside a dirt road leading into a forest. "That's it!"

"You can read it?"

"Not really. I memorized the symbols."

Jack raised an eyebrow.

Penny shrugged. "That and I have an international phone with GPS."

They turned their scooters and went up the road about ten minutes before Jack motioned to Penny to pull over. They rolled their scooters off the road behind the shelter of a large stand of sickly pines.

"What is it, Jack?"

"Let's just re-hash the plan we worked out at the hotel. We're acting like clueless tourists, which I get. But look: we could ride our scooters right into the middle of their camp and say Hi, but that might get us nailed. The idea of setting up a camp nearby and being really obvious is good, because it fits with the clueless thing, but what then? We need to come across them in an accidental way."

"We could pretend to be going for water. Or birdwatching!"

"Yeah, maybe, but I don't know. Wouldn't you think it was suspicious if you were out in the middle of nowhere, planning to kill people, and a couple of ornithology enthusiasts from America showed up?"

"Maybe," she said. "Yeah, I don't know. We really don't have any direction here. Just showing up on scooters is probably better."

"Actually, maybe it is. You've captured the head of some secret society and blown up a hotel, then a couple of Americans ride up on a scooters, one of which prominently featured a stupid cartoon mouse licking its own ear, and you'd be like 'They'd never do that!' "

"Right," she said. "I think the mouse is cute, though."

"You should have said that earlier. I would have switched, 'cause I think it's stupid. But forget that—they're going to be suspicious but they're not expecting us, I guess. We need to use the latter to our advantage. I'd be on high alert if I were these guys. I mean, maybe they already know we're here."

As he said it, there was a crack from above. Jack and Penny looked up and moved just in time to avoid a falling limb.

"Whoa," said Jack, recovering first. "That scared me half to death."

Penny nodded. They were both on pins and needles and the woods were creepy enough without falling limbs.

Taking a deep breath, Jack continued. "Okay, let's just set up a campsite nearby. We have the tents and gear, so let's just pretend we're innocent campers out in the middle of nowhere. We can figure out where they get their water and spy on them there instead of just wandering in. Perhaps they'll leave their compound and we can sneak in. Or go at night and see if we hear anything. With our camp so close, we can pretend it was accidental, and you know, just wave at them and smile if we're caught."

"Sure," said Penny, "that makes sense, but–"

"Whoa," Jack interrupted. "Look at that!" He pointed at the ground where the fallen limb lay. It was turning white as they watched, molding over.

"Weird!" said Penny.

"Yeah, really weird," Jack replied. "The fungi must have rotted it on the tree, but I've never seen mycelium grow that fast."

White threads started to grow towards their scooters as they watched.

"Whoa," Jack said again. "Look at 'em grow."

The strands reached the tire of his scooter and rapidly turned the rubber white. Suddenly the tire exploded with a hiss of air and went flat!

"Penny! Move!" Jack said, pushing her away as the fungus moved towards her shoes. Jack then quickly rolled the second scooter away from the fallen branch.

"What is it doing, Jack!" Penny said as it crept rather from the branch and onto the second tire of Jack's ill-fated scooter. "Oh my goodness! That's freaky!"

The tire exploded seconds later, and they watched in fascination as the fungi crept towards them like frost across a window pane.

"Penny, I think we should get out of here."

Penny nodded. Jack jumped onto the scooter and she sat behind him and they shot back around the pines and onto the road. The mycelium crawled rapidly over the forest floor towards them. Then, as they watched in creeped-out fascination, the threads of fungi reached the road and slowed, apparently unable to move as quickly across the dry, rocky soil as they did across the leaf-covered forest floor.

"It can't eat the road, Penny—it has to pull nutrients from behind it to move. Like a supply chain."

It was moving, though, at perhaps six inches a minute. Jack shuddered. He always appreciated fungi, but this was horrifying. It must be some sort of aggressive Korean slime mold.

"Slime mold," he said to Penny.

"Excuse me?"

"It must be some kind of a slime mold. Normally it looks like vomit, though, or insulation foam sprayed on the ground."

"Nasty!" she said.

"This is more threadlike, but it's gotta be something like a slime mold."

The stuff was now within a foot of their position and was spreading out as if to envelop them both. Jack inched them away and started the scooter.

"I don't like this, Jack," Penny said. "It's freaky."

Jack nodded. "Yeah, freaky. I hope this stuff doesn't grow everywhere. I don't think it can eat us, but I'd hate to be stuck out here without a scooter—Aw SHOOT!"

Jack pointed to the other scooter. The side bags were now white with mold.

"There goes half our supplies!" he said. "I should have yanked the stuff away when I had the chance, before there was a–"

CRACK!

Another branch fell, on the road just behind them. "Jack!" Penny yelled.

Jack looked just long enough to see the branch molding over. Strands of fungi were already moving towards their tires!

"Hang on, Penny!" he yelled. Adrenaline hit him and he gunned the scooter away from the menace, heading deeper into the forest.

"Jack—now I'm actually scared!"

"Me too!" Jack yelled back at her. "This is nuts! What IS that stuff?"

IT IS YOUR ENEMY.

"Hey! It's you!" Jack exclaimed.

"It's me?" Penny said.

"No, not you—the voice in my head." Jack's heart was pounding—he needed answers quickly, and if the voice was going to talk, by golly he was going to talk to it!

"Penny—be quiet for a minute. I need to talk! Listen, Wizard—why are you here now?"

THE DRUG IS IN YOU.

"The drug?"

I HAVE ANSWERED.

"What drug?"

The voice was silent.

"Oh—wait. You mean adrenaline!"

THE DRUG CONNECTS US.

A sudden realization hit Jack. "Okay, that's great, Brown Wizard! Great! That's why you're here only when I'm in a fight. Adrenaline!"

"Jack, this is really, really weird." Penny said.

Jack shushed her.

"Why can't I kill people with lamps?" Jack asked.

YOU CAN KILL A PERSON WITH A LAMP—JUST KILL THEM.

"No, I don't mean a person holding a lamp. I mean that if *I* have the lamp and I throw it with super strength at them, then their bones should shatter as an $18.99 made-in-China Walmart special passes through their body. But it doesn't work that way."

IT WOULD WORK—EVERYTHING IS A WEAPON.

"But it didn't. I tried it. A nice, heavy lamp—yet it only impacted with my normal strength, which wasn't as much as usual because I was beat up. Heck, I'm still beat up. And here I go to face evil Koreans in the middle of the woods with a woman I need to protect as well."

"I heard that!" said Penny. "I can take care of myself!"

Jack shook his head, "Penny, you are less than half as strong as I am. It's just biology. Like, right now I could punch you in the face and kill you."

Her eyes went wide.

"No, it's not a threat—I'm just saying. It's the way things are. Have you ever been punched in the face by a man?"

"No," she said. "No man I hang out with would ever do such a thing!"

"No, of course not. But an enemy might. And look, your jaw—your bone structure—it's just, well, a normal guy, even a weak guy could probably beat you, even though you're in good shape. You need to watch *Filipino Butcher Masters* sometime."

"Well, I don't know about all that, but I did do Krav Maga."

"Great, Penny, you can draw Japanese comics. That will scare them off." Jack had calmed down quite a bit now. The feel of Penny's arms around his waist felt good, too. Even if she was overconfident, it was good having her along.

"So—listen—why couldn't I kill the guy with the lamp?" Jack said.

There was no answer from the voice, but Penny said "Maybe because you weren't strong enough?"

"Shh," Jack said, "I'm talking to the steroid guy. Brown Wizard—tell me—why couldn't I use my strength with a lamp? Why a robe instead? Or reeds? Or a piece of furniture?"

No answer.

"Dang it. He's gone."

Penny patted him on the thigh. "That's good, Jack. Just drive safely. I'm sure the voices in your head will be back soon."

"Penny, I–"

He didn't complete the sentence—directly in front of them there was another CRACK and a large tree fell across the road in a shower of rotten bark and crumbling limbs. Jack slowed, creeping to a halt a couple of feet from the rotten and shattered pine. They'd have to climb over.

He shut off the engine and kicked the kickstand into place, then walked towards the tree with Penny. It was spongy and riddled with insect damage. Other than some old shelf fungi and lichens, there was no sign of the aggressive white mold they'd seen on the other limbs.

"Alright, Penny—it looks okay. Let's drag the scooter over the top."

Penny nodded and jumped the log as Jack rolled the scooter over, standing on top of the log and yanking it over the crumbling wood as Penny put a hand on the front of the little two-wheeler.

As he put the scooter down, the entire log suddenly turned white with mold!

"Yikes!" Jack shrieked, jumping over to Penny's side and jerking the scooter away from the moldering pine. "It's alive!"

"JACK!" Penny yelled. "Your shoes!!!"

Jack looked down—his feet suddenly felt clammy. His boots were white with the stuff—and it was creeping up his pant legs!

"Oh SHOOT!" he yelled, jerking at the laces and pulling off the boots. Beneath them, his socks were also molding. He stripped them off and brushed the mold violently off his pants with his hands. To his great relief, the mold dried to dust and brushed away from the synthetic material.

GOOD JOB, came a voice in his head.

"Good job," Penny said simultaneously. "I thought it was going to eat you!"

Jack looked at his feet—they looked okay, though they were somehow paler than usual. Perhaps the stuff could only feed on dead material, so it ate the socks and shoes? Yet his feet and lower legs felt strange in some way. Then he realized what had happened.

"Sheesh. It ate the hair on my feet and legs."

"Gross!" said Penny.

"Yeah. But it couldn't eat the pants. They're synthetic, so I guess that's too much for the fungi to digest. When it lost its food source, it just died."

THIS TYPE DIES, BUT THERE ARE OTHER TYPES–

"Other types?"

Penny raised an eyebrow at him.

–TYPES WHICH WOULD MAKE YOU LONG FOR DEATH, BUT DEATH WOULD NOT COME.

"Great," said Jack, "I'm starting to rethink this action hero stuff."

Penny nodded. "I know what you mean. Like, I can stand dealing with people and bombs and things—but fungi that eats your hair? That's just way creepy."

Jack turned to her. "Yes, it's way creepy. And it's not natural, I'm sure of that. This is a weapon."

EVERYTHING IS A WEAPON.

"Right—thank you. Whoa, Penny—wait. You called this place 'big mushroom' park, right?"

"Thank you?" Penny said.

"Dang it!" Jack said, "I can't carry on two conversations at once! No—the mushroom, big mushroom park?"

"Yes, that's right."

"Okay, great—we'll get back to that. Just a minute, Penny." He held up a finger to her, then spoke again. "Listen, Brown Wizard—I need to know why the lamp didn't work."

I DO NOT UNDERSTAND.

"The metal lamp—I tried to use my strength on it. Nothing!"

IT WAS NOT PART OF EVERYTHING.

"Wait—how could it not be part of everything?"

The voice was silent. Jack looked over at the log, now a few dozen feet from him, from Penny and the scooter. Yet the fungal threads were creeping toward them over the road, slowly but surely. He shuddered.

"Look—is that log part of everything?"

YES.

"And Penny—is she part of everything?"

"I hope so," said Penny.

YES.

"And the scooter?"

SORT OF.

"Sort of? What do you mean sort of?"

The voice was silent. This was infuriating!

"What about my pants, Wizard? Are my pants part of everything?" Jack snapped in frustration.

Penny winced.

I CAN'T REALLY SEE YOUR PANTS.

"What? You can't see my pants? What are you talking about?"

YOUR PANTS.

"I know you're talking about my pants. But you're saying I'm not wearing pants?" Penny giggled. "It's not funny, Penny! He says he can't see my pants!"

"The fungi couldn't eat them, either," she said.

"Of course!" Jack exclaimed. "Of course! My pants are synthetic. The lamp—it was metal! But the robe, the wooden leg from the love seat, the reeds, even the cop's pants—those were organic. That's it, right? That's what you can use."

I CAN USE EVERYTHING.

"But synthetic or dead materials aren't part of everything. So, it has to be something that is living or was living."

THAT IS WHERE THE ENERGY LIES.

"Great—that's great. So all I need to do is be hopped up on adrenaline and carrying an organic weapon!"

"That's so clichéd, Jack," said Penny. "The organic craze has really gone too far if you're looking for organic weapons. Next thing you'll be telling me you want a fair-trade AK-47."

Jack ignored her and walked to the scooter and pulled out a little hatchet. The blade was metal and the handle was synthetic.

"That's not organic, Jack," Penny said.

"No," said Jack, "But this is."

He walked to the edge of the road and hacked down a small sapling. About a dozen feet from the road there was the sound of a falling limb, but Jack was ready. He'd already jumped back onto the road with his impromptu club by the time the searching mycelial stands reached the stump of the little decapitated pine.

Jack whittled off the small side branches with his hatchet, remembering too late how horrible pine sap can be. He decided not to de-bark the club, as that would really bring out the sap.

"There," he said, looking at Penny. "There's my weapon. I'll be basically unstoppable if I can use it the way I think I can."

He looked around for a rock in the road, picking a jagged one about half the size of a golf ball. He tossed it in the air gently, then swung the pine branch rapidly like a baseball bat, thwacking the rock a good one. It flew about fifty feet before hitting a tree.

"Hmm," Jack said. "That wasn't all that impressive. I don't seem to have it. Can you help me out here?"

"What—you want me to throw a rock to you?" Penny said.

"No, not you. I was talking to the Brown Wizard. Hey, where's my strength?"

There was no answer.

"Aw shucks," Jack said. "He's gone again."

"Uh, Jack, we'd better get gone ourselves. Look!" Penny said.

Jack looked. The strings of fungi were only about six feet from their remaining scooter.

"Yeah, let's git. Big mushroom park. Crazy. At least I don't have to look at the stupid cartoon mouse anymore."

"Yeah, but the rental company will be after us," said Penny.

"True, but we haven't really faced any of the consequences for our actions thus far. Maybe the winning streak will continue."

Jack jumped on the scooter and rolled it away from the slowly creeping white strands. *That is my enemy, the voice had said. The fungi is my enemy. But surely not the only enemy? I mean, what about the Koreans?*

Jack jammed the pine branch into one of the side bags on the scooter and gunned the engine to life as Penny jumped on behind him. His hands stuck unpleasantly to the handles.

I suppose I can worry about the Koreans when we get there, he thought as they cruised down the road.

He thought wrong.

CRACK! A rotten tree fell in the road directly in front of Jack and Penny.

"Oh no, not again!" said Penny.

"Well, I'm already barefoot," said Jack. "I can probably just climb over it and lift the scooter so it doesn't eat the tires."

The log whitened and a pool of mycelium began spreading towards them from beneath it.

"Or maybe not," Jack said.

"Jack—we are in way over our heads. This is insane. We can't save Master Rice. We have no idea what we're doing, really—and I just..."

"What about Cave Manga?"

"Jack—don't make fun of me. I know you're acting cold because I don't care much about plants and I'm really thinking you're insane, but we shouldn't fight each other."

Jack nodded. "You're right. I'm sorry. You're also right that we're in over our heads. No one would fault us for backing out. It's obvious to me that my new-found organization isn't exactly the best equipped or organized, either. They should have known about this stuff. I hate it, but I don't see a way forward."

Penny nodded. Jack took a deep breath. The mycelium were only a few feet from the scooter and slowly creeping closer. With a sigh, he turned the scooter around and started back the way they'd come, frustration constricting his chest. He'd been lousy to Penny, he'd made her think he was insane, he'd failed to reach Master Rice, and now he was going home. James Bond would probably shoot a rope up into the branches and swing them over. Or maybe strip to his boxers and carry the girl and the bike through the mycelium. But maybe my synthetic pants will be like a force field? Or maybe–

CRACK!

Another tree fell across the road in front of them—and they'd only gone about fifty feet from the first one! They were trapped between logs!

CHAPTER SEVENTEEN

The newly fallen pine whitened and rapidly sent mycelial threads creeping onto the road. They were fascinating and unsettling at the same time, like delicate branching white worms. Worms that ate trees, tires and the hair off your legs.

Jack rolled the scooter back to the midpoint between the fallen trees. Thirty feet forwards or backwards and they'd hit the logs. And the safe ground in between was slowly shrinking.

"Jack—what will we do?"

"I'm not sure. If that stuff touches these tires, we'll be walking."

"Barefoot!" Penny exclaimed, then looked down at her jeans. "And if it touches my clothing..."

"Right," said Jack. "We wouldn't want that. No, not at all."

She narrowed her eyes at him.

"What?" Jack said. "It gets cold at night here. And I'm not sharing my marvelously synthetic pants."

Jack scanned the roadsides, thick with fallen leaves and pine needles.

"Could we drive the scooter off the road?" Penny asked.

"Probably," said Jack, "but that stuff seems to be everywhere. It would probably well up from the soil and consume the tires the second we tried. I don't know, though."

Jack rolled the scooter closer to the edge of the road.

"Maybe if we drive fast?" Penny said.

The understory was thin and open. *Maybe.*

Just as Jack made up his mind to go for it, the forest duff close to the tires of the scooter whitened and began growing mycelial strands.

"Oh shoot," Jack said.

"The other side, too, Jack! Look!" cried Penny.

Jack backed the scooter up and turned his head. Sure enough, both sides of the road were whitening as threads roiled onto the rough road and moved their way. As they watched, the gaps between fallen logs and roadside strands were bridged and they were trapped in a rounded and slowly closing rectangle of freakish fungi.

"Jack... if that stuff reaches us..."

Jack nodded. If it reached them, they were going to end up mostly naked, bald and scooter-less. And who knows what it could do long term? It might eat their skin, too.

The road was only about twelve feet wide, and the fungi were reaching in from both sides, eating at least a foot of that width per minute. By Jack's reckoning, they'd be covered in it in less than a quarter hour.

"Should we just run for it, Jack?" Penny asked.

"I don't know, Penny. This is way beyond me. Though maybe if we're barefoot the stuff won't be able to get a hold on anything."

"Yeah," said Penny. "Maybe. But the whole woods seem to be full of it!"

Jack nodded. "Yeah. If there were a spot where we were isolated enough from organic matter... in the middle of a parking lot, for instance, we might be safe."

"What do you mean?" said Penny.

"Well," said Jack, "think of fungi like the internet crossed with a stomach."

"That's totally not making any sense."

"Okay, then think of it more like a series of delicate pipelines, all capable of digestion and transport of materials. It can grow based on what it consumes, reaching out from the food source towards another food source. If it consumes the first before it reaches the second, it just has to stop. Like army supply lines."

There was now only about ten feet of clear road.

"I'll bet those logs are shrinking as it digests them, Penny."

As they watched, the log in front of them slowly sank into the road as the threads spread.

"Wow," Penny said. "It's totally shrinking."

"We need a physical barrier it can't eat," Jack said quietly.

"Well, we can't very well pour a parking lot." Penny crouched down and looked at the advancing strands. "But I wish we could—this is so freaky—Jack—you have to do something!"

She really was scared now. She was holding it together, but Jack could see her trembling. His own heart was racing and his palms were sweaty. The horror of the blind, creeping mass was almost too much. In all directions there was a sea of white. He could actually hear the muffled crumpling of leaves as the mycelial strands digested them in their quest to reach across the pavement towards their human victims. Closer and closer they came, silently closing in. Those strands seemed capable of not just eating their clothing, but creeping over their bodies and maybe even inside of them. Jack imagined himself writhing on the ground inside a choking mass of mycelium, threads creeping into his mouth and ears, down his nasal passages into his lungs...

"God help us," he muttered.

YOU RANG? sounded the professional wrestler voice.

"Oh no," said Jack, "you're not exactly who I was calling for."

"What?" said Penny.

"Shh," said Jack, "it's the voice in my head."

"Ask if he has anything that kills fungi!" Penny said, stepping closer to Jack. They now stood close to each other inside an almost perfect and inexorably narrowing eight foot circle of unhealthy white.

"Listen—Brown Wizard—any ideas?" Jack said.

TRY HER PURSE.

Jack turned to Penny. "Your purse—give me your purse!"

She handed it over without a word and he dug through it.

"Lipstick... probably just wax and colorant. And whoa, Penny, you're loaded. Too bad we can't buy the fungi off. Ah, wait! YES! Hand lotion!"

"Hand lotion?" said Penny. "Does that kill fungi!?"

"This should—look!—jojoba."

"I thought that was some sort of brand-name."

"No, it's a plant oil." *Not that you care about plants,* Jack thought uncharitably.

Jack took the thick tube of lotion and drew an uneven shape around them and the scooter on the hard grit of the road, making sure it was thick and gap-free. He used most of the tube doing so, then carefully spread the line of lotion to about an inch of thickness. The fungi was only a foot from the oily barrier when he finished.

"Penny—take off your shoes."

She did so without question and Jack quickly rubbed some of the lotion on her feet, then did the same with his own.

"Extra insurance," he said. As he did, the first threads of fungi reached the lotion at the point where the scooter's front tire sat in the forward peninsula of the oily shape. Penny grabbed his hand tightly, squeezing so hard it hurt. Jack muttered a prayer under his breath. The threads outside the oil thickened and matted together. It seemed to be stopping at the barrier. The rest of the open road outside the circle whitened. He and Penny now stood hand in hand by the scooter, barefoot on a small island of gray surrounded by a sea of white.

"It's... stopped?" Penny said breathlessly.

Jack nodded. "I think so."

The threads outside continued to thicken. They grew and searched as they moved and intertwined around the circle, like hungry roots licking the sides of a leaking septic tank. Jack's heart was in his throat. If the stuff managed to push over or through...

Penny was now hugging him, shaking. The threads continued to search but didn't seem to be passing through his strange barrier.

"Jojoba forcefield," Jack muttered.

"Good band name," Penny whispered shakily.

Despite himself, Jack laughed. Heart racing, looking possible death in the face, a girl at his side, he felt more alive than he'd ever felt in his life. It was in that moment he realized what a fool he'd been.

Dang the *Dracaena*, full speed ahead.

"Penny?"

She looked up at him.

"I've been a fool."

She nodded.

"No," Jack said, "you're not supposed to just up and agree with me like that. You're supposed to say something like–"

She interrupted him. "Something like, 'Oh Jack, me too.' "

Jack nodded. "You should also say 'I know you're not really crazy just because you have a voice in your head and talk about nasty ice cream flavors.' "

"You still are crazy, Jack. But, shallowly, I like the way you look."

Jack raised his eyebrows, which hurt because of the still-healing cut on his forehead. The fungi's movement seemed to have ceased and all was calm. She was waiting for him to say something.

"I like the way you look, too," Jack said.

"I know," said Penny, batting her eyelids. It looked totally ridiculous. Jack wrapped her in a hug, then decided to press his advantage.

"Penny, may I…"

She pursed her lips, expectantly.

"May I…"

She closed her eyes.

"May I just…"

"Just WHAT, Jack!" she burst out.

"May I explain where jojoba comes from?"

She slapped her hand on his chest.

"Jack!"

Jack laughed, loud and long.

And then the mood broke and their fear rushed back. For outside the circle of white, advancing toward them, were multiple figures in black.

CHAPTER EIGHTEEN

Jack grabbed his stick from the back of the scooter. The men moved silently through the woods to the left, leaving behind footprints in the white mycelium. Jack counted six men, all Korean, all wearing matching business suits. All were untouched by the fungi that came so close to consuming Jack and Penny.

They reached the circle and stood just outside of it. The front-most man bowed.

"I am Park," he said. "Welcome, Mr. Broccoli. And Miss–"

"Wort," Penny said. "Penny Wort."

Jack looked at her, eyes widening. "*Centella asiatica*? You have to be kidding."

The Korean continued before Penny could say anything.

"Miss Wort, how nice. But what is this that you have done?" he said, gesturing at their oily barrier. "This is not respectful."

"Respectful!" Jack exploded. "The fungi was going to eat us!"

"You fear that which you cannot understand. And worse, you have destroyed that which you do understand. There is no innocence in your works. Your baking and grinding. Even your digging. Oh yes—I know about your digging, Jack."

"So?"

"So you have been already judged. However, I have decided to show you a mercy. In fact, you will be given a gift."

"Don't trust him, Jack!" Penny said, unnecessarily. Jack wasn't about to trust this guy. He was too weird.

"Trust, Miss Wort?" said the Korean. "Trust is a human construct, and only a crudeness compared to what I share inside myself, which is far beyond trust."

All the Koreans nodded at exactly the same time. *Now that was freaky*, Jack thought, wondering if they practiced the move in order to be maximally unsettling to park visitors. He remembered there was some sort of Olympic sport where women all did the same moves. *Swimming. Stylized swimming? Maybe the Koreans were on some sort of team like that.*

"Come, though—we must be going," Park continued. "I am sure you are here to see Master Rice."

"Rice!" Penny exclaimed. "You do have him!"

"Of course," said Park. "Now come with us. We will take you to him."

Penny looked at Jack and Jack looked back. Jack considered his chances with the stick against six apparently unarmed Koreans—but realized Penny could be taken hostage while he was fighting. And then of course there was the fungi. It was certain to climb over them if they stepped out. Yet the Koreans had walked over it. Was it their shoes?

"You are concerned about the fungi?" Park said, noting Jack's hesitation.

"Yeah, among other things." Jack said.

"Let me ease your mind," Park replied, shutting his eyes.

As he did, the fungi changed in color, rapidly becoming a grey-green and puffing away into tendrils of smoke in the slight breeze.

"It's burning?" said Penny.

"Sporulating, Miss Wort," Park said mildly. "By the way, it's all over you now." Penny dusted her slacks ineffectually, then realized that keeping microscopic spores off her person was truly impossible.

Oh well, Jack thought. *Gonna have to get some jojoba soap.*

"Let us go now," Park said. "You won't need that stick."

As he said it, the bark of Jack's pine club turned white and he dropped it, brushing his hands off rapidly.

"Come with me," Park ordered.

"May I put my shoes back on?" Penny asked.

Park nodded and she put her shoes back on, then rolled the scooter to the edge of the road. Three men walked behind them, three in front. As they stepped across the road and into the woods, puffs of green-gray dust rose from the ground. Jack glanced back wistfully at Penny's scooter, wishing they were riding it far away from this madness.

Overhead, the canopy of pines felt heavy and thick, as if it were breathing their air. The odor of mold was pervasive. The pine needles prickled uncomfortably beneath Jack's feet, reminding him of his now-devoured footwear.

The walk was a short one. He and Penny had been close to the site just as she'd suspected. A huge clearing opened up before them. The grass beneath their feet was strangely green in patches, though there were rotten trees and stumps here and there. At the edges of the clearing, many trees appeared to be sick. Jack had noticed multiple ill-looking specimens along the path as they'd approached.

Chemicals? he wondered.

To their left was the dome—and to their right, the cabin. It was a simple structure, though it was long and had multiple doors. *Sleeping quarters*, Jack thought. A trickle of smoke from the back denoted the presence of a kitchen as well. As they walked past the cabin, Jack gasped. In front of it sat a vending machine.

A vending machine filled with silvery spheres.

"Souvenirs," smiled Park, noticing Jack's gaze. "Perhaps you can get one later."

Three more Koreans approached Jack and Penny from inside the cabin.

"Hi," Jack said.

"Hello," said the foremost. "I am Park."

"You too!?" Jack said.

"And I am Park." said the Korean on his left. "And I am Park," said the Korean on his right.

"Great," said Jack.

"Come see Master Rice, then I shall do what I must with you," said one of the Parks. He walked towards the dome without looking back. Jack and Penny followed.

As they got closer, Jack noticed something strange about the dome.

"Penny—is it just me or does this thing look uneven to you somehow?"

"Yeah," she said back. "Like it was handmade from mud or something. Not as even as it looked in the pictures."

As they got closer, there was a strong smell of wet earth and leaf mold. Then they were at the edge of the dome. The lead Korean ducked into a wide crack in its side and vanished into the darkness within. Behind Jack and Penny stood eight other men.

Jack put his hand on the structure for a moment and pulled it away. "Whoa—it's cool, and moist. It's like... like a–"

"Mushroom," said Penny. "I think it's a huge mushroom!"

They were herded through the crack into the interior. Around them shone a dim green luminescence. For a moment, they couldn't see much but as their eyes adjusted, their strange surrounding became clearer.

The ceiling above was at least thirty feet high in the center and supported by a thick, white column. The stem of Penny's mushroom, just where it should have been. The walls curving up into the ceiling were deeply lined with dark brown gills.

A pool of water—probably an artificial pond—reflected dimly about ten feet in front of them beneath the central pillar. The room's glow radiated softly from the pillar and the edges of the gills overhead. There was a ripple in the pond and a cloud of bubbles. The Koreans fanned out in a half circle behind Penny and Jack.

From the water's center rose an ancient man, completely bald, wearing a black robe.

"Jack!" said Penny in a sharp whisper. "That's Master Rice!"

"Are you sure?" said Jack.

"Yes, I saw his picture. He wasn't bald in it, but that's definitely him."

"You are correct, Miss Wort," said all of the Parks simultaneously. "That is—or was, I should say—the venerable Master Rice."

The figure now sat on the edge of the pond, looking at Penny and Jack. After a long moment, he spoke. "I knew you were coming."

"You did?" said Jack. "How?"

"I felt it."

"Is that part of your training?" Jack said, impressed.

"It is part of my being," he replied.

"And you are Master Rice?" said Jack.

There was a perfectly synchronized laugh from all the Koreans and the wizened figure.

"Yikes, Jack," Penny whispered. "I feel like we need a crucifix."

"Yeah, no kidding," Jack said, heart racing in his ears.

The figure in front of him spoke again.

"I am Park."

"Wait—you're Park too? You're not—I mean, they said they were taking us to Master Rice."

"Rice I was, now I am also Park."

"Seriously?" Jack said. "Is everyone in Korea named Park?"

Penny nodded. "It seems like it. Did you ever go to Haiti on a mission trip as a teenager?"

"No," Jack said.

"Well I did. Down there, everyone is named Jean."

"Even the men?"

"Everyone," Penny repeated.

"Yeah, but if Rice is now Park it doesn't make any sense. Because he's not even Korean."

"That is correct," said the Master formerly known as Rice.

"It's correct that it doesn't make any sense?" Jack said.

"No," the old man laughed, standing and walking about the pool to them.

"Well I'm confused," said Penny.

The old man reached them and put one of his hands on Penny's shoulder and the other on Jack's. He looked into Jack's eyes.

"It is true that I see you as a murderer and a killer, as a–"

"You do?" said Jack. "You along with every single Korean on the planet!"

"Just the ones named Park so far," said Penny.

"But they're all named Park!"

"Fair point."

"–an adversary," the Master formerly known as Rice continued. "Yet as I am close to you, I can sense something different." He took Jack's hand in his and looked at the nails, then recoiled as if his skin were burned. "Strange, this one."

"Strange?" said Jack.

"Something about your hands, but yes. Unimportant for now. Though perhaps instead of killing you, I could do something else."

"I appreciate that," Jack said. "I really do. Something else is much better. But, uh, look, I don't know what's wrong with you, but Pak send me to rescue you–"

"You ruined my plans for the hotel and for the one called Hardin. You caused me the loss of multiple agents. But now you are here and you are harmless—and you could be useful. As for the girl..."

Two Koreans took hold of Penny's arms. "Hey, let go of me!" she yelped at them as she tried to thrash away, but they only held tighter. She tried to swing her purse at them but it was knocked to the ground.

Jack looked around for a good weapon but there was nothing he could see. As if reading his mind, three Koreans grabbed him as well. The Master formerly known as Rice leaned forward into Jack's face. His breath smelled like a freshly opened carton of *Agaricus bisporus*.

"Now you will see her become Park."

"What?" Jack said. "Wait! No!"

He tried to break free of the Koreans but it was no use. Two more men joined the two already holding Penny. They took her by the arms and legs and lifted her above the ground.

"Jack—help!" she screamed as he watched helplessly. They were going to throw her in the pool. *What is this, some sort of youth group hazing?*

"Now you will see her become Park."

Adrenaline coursed through him. He threw himself against the man to his left, knocking him off balance, then broke his arm free on the other side. He began to swing it around, but it was suddenly stopped by the upraised arm of the Master formerly known as Rice.

Mung fu? Jack wondered—and then the old man closed his hand on Jack's and something very strange happened.

Mycelial threads erupted from both the ground and from the Master formerly known as Rice, covering Jack in white fungi. He struggled against it but they grew too quickly. It was like being wrapped in thick damp shreds of rotten fabric.

"You will stay, Jack," said the man he had been sent to rescue. "And watch the birth of oneness."

"Jack!" Penny yelled again. "What did they do to you! What did they–"

But her voice was cut off as the four men tossed her unceremoniously into the pool.

Bubbles rose, but Penny did not. Nine Parks and the Park formerly known as Rice silently faced the pool.

"Stop it, Rice, stop it! Get her out!" Jack yelled. But there was no answer.

The Koreans had released Jack when the fungal net had wrapped around him. Jack was trapped, half-hunched over and entwined in a grotesque mass of white. He had a thought and spoke it out loud. "Where are you, Brown Wizard?"

There was no answer. *Was the fungi was too powerful? Was it having an effect on his mind even now?*

The Koreans watched the pool in silence. How long had she been in there? She must be almost dead!

Jack realized that he could still move his feet and his hands. That was strange. In fact, as he slipped them around a little, they became looser. He struggled, finally managing to free one of his legs along with his right arm. Unnoticed, he hooked Penny's purse with his toes and drew it to himself. There was still a little lotion left. *And if these men were controlled by the fungi...*

All of the men around him were still silent, as if completely lost in concentration on the pool. Jack grabbed Master Rice by the shoulder and spun him around. His eyes were empty, as if faraway in thought. Jack pried the man's jaw open with one hand. It stayed open.

"Here goes nothing," he said, then grabbed the lotion tube from Penny's purse and squeezed it into the old man's mouth.

For a moment, nothing happened. Then the man lurched forwards, falling to the ground, thrashing and twitching, eyes scrunched shut, mouth open in a rictus of pain. He shuddered violently, then went limp.

Shoot... I killed him, Jack thought.

Then Jack noticed the rise and fall of his chest. He was still breathing. But his comrades hadn't noticed his fall—they were still concentrating on the lake. Jack pulled against the remaining threads and they started to break. *I have to get to the lake.*

Suddenly, the Master formerly known as Rice regained consciousness and looked up.

"What– Where am I?"

"Surrounded by crazy Koreans—and my girlfriend is in that lake! I need to get her," he said, finally snapping free.

"No!" Rice gasped, "Do not go in the lake!"

"Listen, you crazy freak—I don't have time for this."

Master Rice grabbed him. "I am free of the Park—trust me, if you go in that lake you will surely fall before them. That is the quickest way to free Parking." His grip was strong, despite his frail appearance.

"But—dang it all to heck, man—she's gotta be dead now. I blew it! They took her from me!"

"That they did," said Master Rice. "But she is not dead."

"She isn't? How can you even–"

An explosion of bubbles came from the lake and a pair of slender arms emerged, followed by a bald head.

"Penny!" Jack yelled.

She climbed onto the shore, wrapped in the tattered remnants of her clothes, and she hacked and vomited up a prodigious quantity of what appeared to be swamp water. After a few minutes of gagging and heavy breathing, she stood and looked at Jack. Her face was blank, showing no sign of the extroverted Penny he knew. He baldness made her appear even more alien. Even her eyebrows were gone.

The Koreans also turned to look at him. Their trance had apparently broken with the emergence of the girl.

"Hello, genocidal one," she spoke.

"Geno— Wait, you're the one that kills plants!"

"That is not me—I only kill that which must die to save that which must live."

"Penny..."

She smiled slowly, and walked to Jack, dripping water. She smelled of fungi.

Then she looked him directly in the eye. "You may call me Park."

CHAPTER
NINETEEN

Jack was aghast as Penny stood before him. *It's like someone else is wearing her body,* he thought. And then: *That is exactly what's happening.*

Beside him, Master Rice stood quietly. On casual inspection he appeared to be in a resting position but Jack knew from his studies on YouTube that the man was in a pose meant for rapid striking against an enemy.

Jack tried to reason with the unsettlingly bald girl. "Penny, you can't be a Park. You're not even Korean. If I had to guess, I'd say you were mostly Anglo-Saxon with maybe some German mixed in."

"And at least 5 percent fungi," said Master Rice in a low voice.

Penny shrugged. "I am Park."

Jack frowned. "Okay, I'm really getting tired of the Park thing. It's ridiculous. It's…"

"It is correct," said Master Rice.

"Yeah?" said Jack. "I don't get it. I get that it's a common Korean name, but you were Park a few minutes ago, all these guys are Park, the guy in the hotel, the one that took Hardin, look, it just defies probability, plus people are just piling on and taking the name. It's silly. How is it even vaguely correct to call her Park? Or you, a few minutes ago, before I gave you a lotion smoothie?"

Master Rice smacked his lips. "Ah, that is the flavor in my mouth. It is unpleasant."

"Yeah, well, you were being unpleasant. It was a long shot."

"Jojoba?" Master Rice asked.

"Very good," Jack nodded. "Natural fungicide. Now tell me about the name Park."

"It is not merely Park the name. It is Park the place."

Jack frowned. "I don't get it. Park the place? Park the–"

Master Rice nodded. "This place. This Park. They are all part of it."

Penny bowed.

"Wait a minute, you are *the* park? Like, Big Coon Ale Park?"

"Big Mushroom Park, I think you would translate it," said Master Rice.

"Right, that's right," said Jack. He looked at Penny.

"Penny, don't you remember me? Are you in there?"

She smiled. "I remember all, and I encompass all."

Jack noticed that all the Koreans' mouths moved in tandem with hers. *Creepy.*

"Do you remember that you like me?" Jack said. "Maybe even love me?"

Penny looked blankly back at him.

"Don't you want to let us go, Penny?" Jack pressed. "Don't you want to leave with me?"

"No," she replied. "I wish to kill all those who threaten us worldwide."

"Threaten us?"

"Yes, us. All we have to lose is our chains."

"Chains? Who is we?"

Penny shook her head. "You have no idea, which is why you must die."

"Penny!"

She cocked her head.

"Or perhaps you might prefer to take a swim?"

Suddenly, Jack felt himself shoved violently forwards. He tried to hold back but there was nothing he could grab.

In horror, he fell headlong into the pond and was rapidly drawn down into the water by some sort of grasping tendrils.

Down and down he went, struggling to hold the air in his lungs. His skin tingled and it felt like something was growing into his ears and nose.

Suddenly there was a feeling of detachment and Jack realized he was looking at his body from a distance. There he floated in the water, some ten feet beneath the surface, thrashing about. Jack could feel a greater mind around him. It had pushed him out of his own brain! The last time something like this had happened was when he and Drew were taste-testing tequilas at a new Mexican lounge place, and Drew had said, "Now let's try the Mezcal." They had, and then gone on to a selection of silvers, and then Jack remembered watching himself dancing with a rather dumpy Mexican grandmother on top of a table. There had been some Coronas, an impromptu tortilla-making competition, and a trip in a low-rider. It was all like watching a movie in fast-forward, though, his entire self displaced by the agave gods and his corporeal form turned over to a frantic fiesta of frolic. This was like that, except without any Mariachi music. And he was apparently watching himself drown, instead of watching himself get a little too touchy with a Mexican abuela.

"Get out of my head!" Jack said from afar. All he felt was a vast malevolence. He saw the air gasp out of his lungs and fungal strands reach into his thrashing body. Far away, he felt it as well, but couldn't do anything about it.

"Help me—oh God help me," he gasped as he watched.

I'M BACK, said a way-too-loud voice.

"You're not God!" said Jack, "But thanks—where the heck were you?"

WORKING IN THE GARDEN.

"Ah, makes sense. Great. I tried to call you earlier."

SORRY.

"As you can probably see, I am drowning right now and my body has been taken over by a giant sentient fungus."

YES, THIS IS NOT GREAT. IT IS A POWERFUL THING YOU HAVE RUN INTO. LET ME THINK.

"Think fast—I might be drowned by now. That doesn't look good," Jack said, attempting to gesture with a non-existent arm towards his still form, wrapped in fungi.

YOU'RE STILL ALIVE, OR ELSE I WOULD NOT BE TALK-ING TO YOU NOW.

"Well, that's a good point," said Jack. "I suppose I'd be handed a harp right now if I were dead."

YES, I ASSUME SO. THEY DON'T LET ME IN UP THERE.

"Great. Here I am, drowning to death and consorting with demons right before meeting St. Peter. That is great, just great."

SHHH, I HAVE AN IDEA.

"An idea? What kind of idea–"

Suddenly Jack was looking out of a different pair of eyes. He was beside the pond, next to the possessed Penny, surrounded by a group of silent Koreans, all of whom were focused on the pond.

He looked down at his arms. They were thin and wiry. Wait—he was—he was inside Master Rice?

"Master Rice?" he said.

"Yes?" came a voice. "Who is this?"

"It's Jack," he said. Or thought. It wasn't really clear.

AND I AM HERE AS WELL.

"Who are you?" came Master Rice's voice, obviously alarmed at the second intruder into his brain.

"That's my friend the Brown Wizard," said Jack, as if that helped. "Though where's Penny? If my consciousness left my body and went into Master Rice, where did she go?"

I AM NOT SURE.

Master Rice shook his head. "My own consciousness was lost in the pool when they took me. I do not understand how you got out."

"I don't either," Jack said.

I HAVE PRESERVED THE CARETAKER.

"Ah. Thank you." Jack said—or thought—to Master Rice. "We need to fight, Master Rice. Think you can grab Penny and get out of here before they break their trance?"

"What about you? Your body is still in the pool."

HE WILL BE OKAY FOR NOW.

Master Rice nodded and looked around.

EVERYTHING IS A WEAPON.

"Every thing may be a weapon," Master Rice thought back at Jack and his protector, "but I have no things. I will have to kick them, while they are concentrating."

"Just grab something organic, Master Rice," Jack said. "In case they wake up. Grab anything. The Brown Wizard will make it deadly."

Jack felt Master Rice's body course with a surge of adrenaline as the old man focused himself.

GOOD, THAT HELPS.

The Mung Fu master walked deliberately to the wall of the room and broke off a large hunk of mushroom.

"Will this work?" he asked.

YES, THAT IS GOOD. NOW HIT SOME PEOPLE.

Master Rice didn't need to be told twice.

He swung the hunk of fungi over his head in the traditional "sickle for tall rice" movement and knocked nine entranced Koreans to the ground, spattering mushroom paste all over the place.

"I could get used to this," he said, wiping his hands on the ground. Penny was still staring towards the pond, oblivious.

"Now what?" Master Rice asked.

Before anyone could answer, Jack's now-possessed form emerged from the pond, bald and dripping. The girl formerly known as Penny blinked, looked at the fallen men around her, then looked at Master Rice.

"You!"

"Sorry, Park," Master Rice said as he hefted a hunk of mushroom and smacked her on the head. She crumpled, and he caught her, laying her carefully down beside the fallen Parks.

Then Master Rice turned and looked at Jack, which meant that Jack was also looking at Jack, watching himself violently retch up water. Jack was glad he wasn't inside Jack's body at the moment.

"Well, Master Rice. You have disabled some of my vessels," said the Park who was now Jack.

Master Rice bowed. "I was obliged to do so, yes. Your microcentrism is both dangerous and distasteful."

The pseudo-Jack walked closer to Master Rice. From outside, Jack thought his body actually looked pretty good. Especially considered he'd just drowned.

"Why do you seek to stop me?" Park said with Jack's mouth.

"You murder with impunity. You care nothing for life."

"Life! You speak to me of life?" Park laughed an unpleasant laugh. "The amount of life destroyed by men on a daily basis is staggering. They may set up organizations to save the seals, or egg whales, or striped owls, or any number of their precious multicellular pets—yet they overlook all the teeming single-celled lives, and all the rich tendrils of fungi that bind together the earth. The life of the soil."

"Primitive life," Master Rice said. "Unthinking life."

"Unthinking! Unthinking! Do you call me unthinking?"

"Master Rice," Jack asked from inside Master Rice's mind, "what is he?"

"He is an ancient creature, Jack. A fungi which has now become not only sentient, but dangerous."

"Like—a honey mushroom?" Jack said. "The dead trees all around here, the mycelium—that's all him!"

"Correct," thought Master Rice. "He has consumed acres."

"But what about the Koreans? The Agents of F.A.D.A.M.?"

"Tools, nothing more," said Master Rice. "Though I would like to know where they first came from." He spoke aloud to the fungus-mind wearing Jack's body. "You are obviously a thoughtful creature. I apologize."

Park looked at him silently through Jack's eyes. A group of eight more men entered through the crack in the mushroom. This time they were armed. Each one carried a spading fork, tines sharpened to needle points.

Park spoke again with Jack's voice.

"Humans have a dim understanding of the life in the soil. This pond behind me, for instance. Do you know what makes it so powerful?" Master Rice shook his head.

"Diversity. Unity in diversity. It is teeming with a variety of life, of which I am dominant. In simple terms, it is a rich bacterial and fungal ecosystem, perfectly balanced and raised into life from what men would call 'leaf mold'."

"Leaf mold?"

"A crude term. Like calling London 'organized rock pile', but it must do."

"So the pond is a leaf mold culture?" said the real Jack inside Rice's mind. "That's crazy. There are a bazillion kinds of creatures inside of leaf mold. Is Park actually some sort of gestalt organism?"

"I will ask," Master Rice thought back at him, then turned to Jack's possessed body. "Are you some sort of gestalt organism, Mr. Park?"

Jack's body bowed. "I am now. And as you can see, I even incorporate multicellular animal aspects into my nature."

All the Koreans snapped their forks out in front of their bodies in a single fluid motion. All the tines pointed at Master Rice.

"You made a mistake, Park." Master Rice said mildly. "Your attacks you may see as only more basidia beneath your cap, but humans do not take kindly to being controlled."

"I care not how kindly mankind takes being controlled! I act only in self-defense!"

"No," said Master Rice. "That you do not. You kill soil scientists, technicians, professors. Even agricultural salesmen! Your murders rise in heaps to your gills!"

"I destroy those who destroy good life."

"You destroy even those who do not attack you. Before you overextended your hyphae, we did not know what you were. Now we do." He gestured to the fallen Koreans. "Your annulus constricts already. The universal veil falls from our eyes."

"You fool," Park snapped. "I am older than you and much more powerful. I will feed upon your carbon!"

"As you fed upon the trees you destroyed?"

"All must eat!"

Master Rice shook his head. "Did not the trees have a right to live? You have outgrown your volva, Park."

Without warning, the ring of fork-wielding Koreans charged at Master Rice.

"JUMP!" a voice yelled, and Master Rice jumped, backflipping over the closest Korean and racing around the pool.

"You can't fight them all!" Jack said. Master Rice did not reply, but he put his back against the central stalk of the giant mushroom and faced down eight Koreans and Jack's fungally animated form.

GRAB THE STALK! PLUCK THE MUSHROOM!

The Koreans were almost on top of Master Rice. He gave a mighty yank at the stalk, hooking both hands into its watery flesh and pulling hard. There was a spongy snap, and it collapsed, and the roof started to fall.

"You'll smoosh Penny!" Jack thought loudly. "And my body!"

But the light and spongy mushroom tissues rained down lightly in an earthy crumble of wet fungi, freeing them from the unearthly dome. Master Rice dug up through the mess, then stood on the squishy surface as the Koreans and Jack's mushroom-maddened body also broke free. Chunks of mushroom floated soggily in the pond.

"Can you think that by destroying my fruiting body you have destroyed me?" Park shrieked in Jack's voice. "I cannot be taken with such a simple trick."

Mycelial strands burst from the fallen mushroom like mold on a loaf of Ezekiel bread, shooting up Master Rice's legs. He spun rapidly, kicking away the strands, but every time his feet came down, they came twining back.

"Any ideas, Jack?" Master Rice gasped, as he narrowly dodged the tines of a thrown spading fork and roundhouse-kicked its former owner in the motion known in Mung Fu as "stalk of winter grain falling without warning in sudden wind". He was dancing wildly about the crushed pieces of mushroom and wouldn't last much longer. The mycelial strands kept tripping up his feet while the Koreans attempted to skewer him with their forks.

Jack wracked his disembodied brain. Something nagged at him. A memory—something unexpected—perhaps the answer to their plight. Jack's possessed body picked up the fallen fork and entered the fray. There was something Jack needed to remember about his stolen body. Something in his pocket!

"Master Rice! Pick my pockets!"

Master Rice grabbed Jack's body, spun him around, snaked hands into both of its pockets, then kicked it into a group of advancing Koreans.

"No help! What am I looking for here?" he asked. "You have coins, one mint, and a packet of–"

"Yeast!" Jack yelled in Master Rice's mind. "Open the yeast! Throw it in the pool!"

"Okay, whatever you–"

But Master Rice never finished his sentence, as three Koreans slammed into him at the same time, knocking him to the ground, and the mycelium began creeping over his body. He struggled, and another Korean drove a spading fork at his chest. Master Rice freed one arm and deflected the blow, but one of the tines went through the palm of his hand—and the packet of yeast held in it.

With a yell of pain, he yanked the hand back, unbalancing the man with the fork, who fell headlong into the pool. He looked at the punctured and bloody packet of yeast—and he threw it into the pool after his flailing attacker.

"You only prolong your death, Master Rice," Jack's body said. It stood over Master Rice's prostrated and whitening form with a spading fork in his hand. "You will soon know what it is to be a victim!"

Master Rice could not answer. The mycelium had wrapped around him completely and were squeezing out his life. "Master Rice!" Jack said inside his head. "Come on! You must be able to break free."

"I cannot, Jack. In case you hadn't noticed, I am suffocating at the moment!"

"Brown Wizard! Can you help him?" Jack thought, but there was no answer. *Is he gardening again? Right now?*

"Now you will know what it is like to be turned and torn, Master Rice!" Park said in Jack's voice, lifting his wickedly sharp fork. Around him, a circle of Koreans brandished their own forks, all pointed towards the paralyzed Mung Fu master.

And then they quavered for a moment.

"What is this?" said the chorus of Park. "The balance, it is wrong. Something is wrong!"

"The threads are loosening a little, Jack," Master Rice gasped.

The human components of Park looked disoriented. Jack's body shook his head, as if to clear it. Penny was still somewhere beneath the mushroom. Jack hoped she was able to breathe.

"We must purge the invading organism," Park said. "We must..."

Then Jack's body and all of the fork-wielding Koreans looked up in an uncannily synchronized motion. "Wait—what is that?" Park said, a note of fear in its voice. "An engine?"

Through Master Rice's eyes, Jack saw a black Antonov An-2 appeared over the tree line, a spray of mist emerging from the array of emitters on the bottoms of the wings.

"What is that!?" Park yelled with Jack's body. *Do I really sound that petulant normally?* Jack thought. *I need to work on making my voice deeper.*

The mist roiled over them as the plane dashed above the clearing. Suddenly there was screaming, coming from everywhere. Jack watched his body fall to the ground, writhing in pain. The Koreans were doing the same, dropping their forks and flailing about in agony.

The mycelial strands melted away into black goo, releasing Master Rice, who was too weak to do anything but lay on the ground and gasp, blinking away the painful substance that had been sprayed from above. Between blinks, Jack looked upwards at the blue heavens—then suddenly, he was looking up from a completely different location.

What in the world? he thought. And then Jack realized where he was—back in his own body. *Park was gone. Something in the spray must have pushed him out!*

Jack heard the plane coming back on another pass. He tasted a disgusting metallic flavor in his mouth. It was like sucking on a mouthful of dirty pennies. He spit and rolled over. His eyes stung with it, and he was half-blind.

"Penny!" he yelled, jumping up and sloshing through the rapidly dissolving mushroom and dodging the bodies of fallen men. "Penny!"

Then he saw her through the chemical-induced tears running down his face. She was covered in goo, and she was still out cold.

He rushed to her side, falling more than once in the slippery gunk, and he pulled her onto his lap and brushed goop off her face with his hand. She was breathing—he had been so afraid she was going to suffocate amidst the decaying fungus. He hugged her to him, held her hand, and prayed he'd never lose her again.

CHAPTER TWENTY

"Copper sulfate, Jack," Pak said. "An oldie but a goodie."

"Not a goodie for organs, though," said Master Rice. "I recommend everyone run through a course of plant-based acupuncture."

"Not chelation therapy?" Jack asked. "I knew this guy once who had mercury poisoning. They chelated him."

Master Rice shrugged. "I am of the old school, Mr. Broccoli."

A Korean nurse appeared with a bowl of soup and set it on the table beside Jack's hospital bed and winked at him. He winked back. She then left for a moment and returned with a kettle from which she poured three cups of fragrant tea.

Master Rice thanked to her and then turned to Jack and motioned at the soup. "For now, I suppose, you may let your food be your medicine."

The soup was a broth containing small green bits and much larger black bits.

"What is this stuff?"

Pak and Master Rice talked back and forth in Mandarin for a moment.

"I think the closest translation would be 'black fungus soup', Jack. Very good for you."

"I don't think so. I've got a fungal hangover," Jack replied.

"It's hair of the mushroom, Jack," Pak said.

"Couldn't you guys just send in a steak? Oh—and some *Ocean Octaves!*?"

Pak smiled patronizingly and shook his head no. It was good to see him shake his head without wincing, even though Jack wanted to punch the smile off his smug face.

They had been sitting by his bedside for the last hour, going over what had happened in Big Mushroom Park. Jack had arrived at Penny's side just moments before a Korean special ops team and three of Master Rice's men showed up to secure the area. The fallen Korean puppets used by Park had been brought around, Master Rice had been resuscitated, and everyone had been stripped, sprayed down, then soaped up and rinsed repeatedly with clean water to remove the copper sulfate from their bodies. Jack remembered the unpleasant sensation of the running water his rescuers had poured over his eyes, again and again. Then there was the trip to the hospital and another round of scrubbing and eye-washing. *Only marginally better than going blind*, he thought. He'd been here for a couple of days. His body was weak but he felt about ready to get home. *Man alive, James Bond never spend this kind of time in the hospital*, he thought.

"How's Penny today?" he asked Pak.

"Other than the bruise on her head, she is well."

"Yeah," Jack said. "Master Rice smacked her on the head. Not very chivalrous."

"Normally I am, but she was not really herself that day," Master Rice replied.

Jack looked at the two of them as they peacefully sipped their tea. This had been the weirdest week of his life. The ordeal seemed to be over but something was still bugging him.

"Look, Pak... why did you guys just let Penny and me wander in there to rescue Master Rice? Why didn't you just go in and fungicide the place?"

Pak pursed his lips. "Well, we weren't sure we really wanted to destroy him."

"Park?"

"Yes. He was a very interesting case. A fungi which reached sentience. You do not simply kill a creature like that."

"Come on, Pak," Jack retorted. "He was trying to kill us. He was sending agents around the world to hunt people down. Remember Hardin?"

"Unlike you, Jack, I prefer to move slowly. We wished to know if he could be reasoned with." Pak shrugged. "You are a tiller, not one who waits for balance of soil web. We are more holistic."

Jack rolled his eyes. "So you sent me in there to smoke him out?"

"In a sense," Master Rice said. "I had a microphone transmitter on my person. All of Park's words were recorded. Before I was forcibly converted, I tried to reason with him. However, we were literally Kingdoms apart."

"And your people still let us go in?" Jack said.

Pak nodded. "They figured you would keep Park confused until we could organize a proper rescue—you did much better than that, though. You are a strange man, Jack. Full of possibilities."

Jack gestured at the soup. "You people eat this stuff. And you think I'm strange?"

"Well," said Master Rice, "you have a crazy voice in your head. And you are addicted to a snack food. I have also heard that you eat random food in alleys without taking precautions against poisoning. And you thought a brainwashed Korean was your mom. And–"

"Okay, I get the point." Jack sighed. "At least it's over now. I suppose I need to look for another job, then–"

He stopped as the door opened.

"Penny!" said Jack as she walked in unsteadily. Pak stood and offered her his chair. She wore a hat over her bald head. It made her look young and vulnerable. She collapsed into the offered chair.

"Good to see you, Master Rice, Pak... and Jack. Oh, Jack, I'm sorry."

"Sorry about what?" he said.

"Sorry about the *Dracaena*."

"The *Dracaena*—your plant?"

"Yes, you were right."

"I was?"

"Yes," she replied. "I looked it up. It was a *Dracaena*."

"Was?" he said.

"Yes," she said, carefully avoiding his eyes. "It's, uh..."

"It's what?" he said.

"It's dead."

"Dead?" he replied. "How do you know it's dead?"

She sucked her lip. "Well..."

"Did you phone home? Did you have a sitter who called and gave you the bad news?"

She shook her head.

"Could you sense its death from here? I mean, I swear—sometimes I just know when a plant is dying..." he trailed off.

"No," she said. "It died last year."

"Last year? But–"

"I couldn't bear to tell you, Jack. See, I realized at some point that I really liked you. I mean, really *really* liked you. And I know plants are your entire life, and I wanted to be a part of that life, and I figured if I told you that you'd hate me forever. But the guilt of it, and the way you came to my side—they told me about it, how they found you holding me while I was still unconscious, and that all you asked about was my health, even though you'd been possessed by a giant fungus, and..."

A tear rolled down her cheek as she continued. "I just, I just couldn't live a lie. I came here to tell you that I, well, I'm a plant killer."

She buried her head in her hands and sobbed.

"Penny..." Jack said, shocked. The two Chinese men were silent.

"Penny," he said, then continued with the thirteen hardest words he'd ever said in his life. Fourteen, if you count the contraction as two words. "I don't care about the *Dracaena* as much as I care about you."

She looked up at him, eyes wide, blinking away tears.

"You don't!? And you do?"

Jack nodded, and said the six next hardest words he'd ever said. "No, it was just a plant."

"Oh Jack!" she said, then stood up. "Oh Jack!" she repeated, then kissed him.

Jack kissed her back, hard. He loved this girl, he knew it, and he never wanted to see her possessed by anything other than himself ever again. A flood of adrenaline raced into his system.

EVERYTHING IS A WEAPON, said the voice inside his head.

"Oh, not now!" he said.

Penny pulled away, embarrassed, and Jack realized he had spoken out loud. "Oh, no, actually, sorry Penny, it's just the—oh never mind," he said, then pulled her back for a second kiss.

When he finally let go, he realized he and Penny were alone in the room.

"So," he said. "It looks like we're going to be together for a long time."

She nodded.

"Excellent. I've got some seed catalogs you absolutely need to see."

"I'd like that, Jack," she said.

"Really?" he said.

She hesitated just a moment too long.

Jack frowned at her playfully. "Penny, don't make me drop you in a vat of sentient leaf mold again."

They broke into laughter as she hugged him fiercely.

EPILOGUE

It was a bright Sunday afternoon. A solitary figure walked across the grass at Lee Memorial Park towards a recently dug grave.

The man removed his baseball cap, revealing a stubbly head, then unwrapped a package.

Inside was a book. He somberly set it on the grave and laid his hand on the tombstone.

"I did it," he spoke quietly. "I did what you asked."

It was hard to believe that a force of personality as strong as Hardin's could be gone from the world so quickly.

Dilbert's face stared up at him from the book lying on the recently turned earth.

"I wanted you to approve of me, boss. This book was going to be a gift. I thought we'd be reconciled, you know, and then I'd have a few 'get out of trouble free' cards in case I busted anything else expensive. I had no idea that instead I would end up defeating a gigantic sentient fungus in your name."

He patted the grave stone a last time and walked back to his car, remembering his boss and his former life. It all seemed so far away.

Even the sycamore/fig controversy didn't matter that much anymore. Jack had attended morning services and he had gotten some strange looks because of his missing eyebrows and hair, but they were nice country people, and they left him alone. After the service, he caught his pastor for a moment and shared with him the difference between *Ficus sycomorus* and *Platanus occidentalis*. The pastor seemed to understand and promised to recant his mistake at the beginning of next week's service. Jack was impressed. He considered asking him about the voice in his head but decided that was probably not a good idea as of yet.

Jack got into his car and drove home. Penny was busy, but they were supposed to meet later in the week. For now he was on his own, with no boss, no job and no real responsibilities. That meant he'd finally get to spend some serious time in the garden.

He stepped inside, grabbed a Celery Stout from the fridge and a half-empty stale bag of *Ocean Octaves!* from on top of it, then settled into his favorite chair. As he sat down, he suddenly heard a bubbling sound. Worried something horrible was happening with his internal organs, he stood up again. The bubbling sound continued. It was coming from the other room. No—wait—that sounded like Pak's–

"Jack! You are home. And you are lazy!"

Yep, it was Pak.

"Look, Pak... I'm kind of tired right now."

"No time for that, Jack. How'd you like to be a full-on international gardening spy of mystery? Maybe even with actual training this time?"

Jack suddenly felt every ache and pain in his body acutely. Then he remembered he hated working a real job more than he hate being beaten up.

"Order my tux, Pak. I'm ready."

Printed in the USA
CPSIA information can be obtained
at www.ICGtesting.com
BVHW030917010923
669009BV00001B/2